S0-BFC-147

Vision in the Waves

Out in the water, a silvery shape flashed across the waves. For a moment Bonnie stared after it, open mouthed, trying to decide what she had seen. It was gone so quickly she couldn't be sure, but her mind formed the image of a hand and part of a slender white arm. The arm was draped in a long drift of lacy weed tipped in pinks and yellows and blues and greens. Fingers with glinting silver nails had been grasping the peaks of the waves as they sped toward shore, and the waves' white caps looked like the long, flowing hair of a woman.

Bonnie's heart was hammering so hard that she pressed one fist against her chest. Beneath her clenched fingers, she could feel her grandmother's pearl, smooth and round against her skin. Was it warmer suddenly, or was it her imagination? The sound of Bobbie's calling crept into her consciousness, and she turned toward her alarmed friend.

"Bonnie! Bonnie!" cried Bobbie. "What did you see? What did you SEE?!"

The Secret of Mermaid Island

By Judith Wade

Published by Riley Press, Eagle, Michigan

This book, including names, characters, places and
events, is a work of fiction.

Cover photography by Karen Patterson
http://www.karenpattersonphoto.com/

Rileydog image by Tina Evans, Artist

Some images copyright www.clipart.com

Copyright 2003, 2008 Loraine Hudson
All rights reserved

ISBN 978-0-9728958-0-4
0-9728958-0-9

Published in the United States of America by Riley
Press, P.O. Box 202, Eagle, MI 48822
http://rileypress.hypermart.net

I

To Sarah, my mermaid girl, for her ideas, her help, her enthusiasm and her love.

1

"Mermaid Island is a stupid name," said Bonnie Campbell sourly, kicking her sandaled foot at a pebble that had rolled across the deck of the ferry. "Why would anyone name an island that?"

She looked glumly across the tossing, white-crested waves at the distant shore, its line of trees growing steadily closer as the boat chugged across the open water. Her mother laid her hand on Bonnie's shoulder and squeezed it gently.

"Mermaid Island is a beautiful place," she said. "I loved it as a child, and now that I'm coming back to do my research, it's like a dream come true for me!"

Bonnie looked guiltily at her mother's glowing face, then turned her eyes sadly back to the water. Her mother had never been happier, but Bonnie's summer was stretching out ahead of her like a long, lonely tunnel. No trips to the shopping mall; no movies; no school dances with her friends. Why couldn't she spend the summer having fun like her friends were?

Amelia's family was going to Boston, and Laura and her two sisters were heading for SummerDaze amusement park next week. Laura had invited Bonnie to go to SummerDaze with them, but the Campbells' travel plans had interfered.

"I'd rather be anywhere than Mermaid Island," thought Bonnie, feeling more and more depressed.

What would she do while her mother tramped around the woods looking for endangered plants and writing notes for her research paper?

Bonnie sighed, but she tried not to do it too loudly. Her mother had folded her slender body into one of the deck chairs and was looking joyfully at the island as the dock drew near, the wind whipping her short blonde hair around her face.

If only Bonnie could feel some of that same excitement!

The ferry bumped to a stop and the crew began driving cars down from the deck while the passengers stepped onto shore. Caro Campbell, Bonnie's mother, lugged her laptop computer, a brief case and her camera down the ramp, while Bonnie tagged along behind, toting her backpack and eyeing the people waiting along the dock.

Most of them appeared to be retired couples who probably had summer cottages on Mermaid Island. There were no teenagers, and no one paid any attention to Bonnie as she and her mother loaded their things into their station wagon.

Caro Campbell slid behind the wheel of the car and Bonnie climbed in next to her, settling her backpack on the seat. She touched the pearl hanging on its gold chain around her neck. It had belonged to Bonnie's grandmother, and Bonnie thought back to the old woman's words as she gave the necklace to Bonnie.

"This necklace is very special, Bonnie," her grandmother had whispered in her sweet, soft voice. "The pearl came from an oyster with a shell of flawless silver, who lived in the bluest part of the ocean. You can still see the ocean in the pearl, if you look closely. And feel how warm it is? A perfect pearl always feels warm to the touch."

She closed Bonnie's fingers around the necklace and held her hand gently. "Now the pearl is yours, my darling. It's been in our family for many generations. May it bring you all the joy a special young woman like you deserves."

Bonnie's eyes misted over for a moment, and she turned her face toward the car window. Her grandmother had passed away last year and Bonnie still missed her terribly.

The car rolled down a short city street, and Bonnie caught sight of a sign for the local library. Her spirits rose slightly, and she blinked her tears away. A library! That's the first place she would go. An island with a library couldn't be all bad. She turned and smiled at her mother, and when her mother smiled back Bonnie felt a little bit better.

"Honestly, Bonnie Campbell," she told herself sternly. "Try to make an effort for your mother's sake. This research project is the most important thing in the world for her. Don't ruin her summer just because you're feeling sorry for yourself!"

With that thought, Bonnie turned back to the car window, just in time to see a red-haired girl skip around the corner of the library building and out of sight. Bonnie craned her neck to see where she had gone, but she had disappeared.

At least the island had one other person her age, Bonnie thought.

She leaned back in her seat as her mother drove out of town and then turned the car into the driveway of the little cottage that was to be their summer home.

The next couple of hours were spent unloading boxes and suitcases and organizing their belongings. Bonnie fell in love instantly with her little upstairs bedroom. It had a dormer with a window seat that faced the street, and she had a clear view of a pretty garden by the house next door. Bonnie went out to the station wagon and brought in another load.

"Where do you want the computer, mom?" she called.

She rounded a corner and nearly crashed into her mother, who was standing on a stool peering into the linen closet. She steadied herself by holding onto a shelf and glanced down at Bonnie.

"Put it in the little corner room, the one with the windows that face south and west. I like to watch the waves in the evening. Did you see the pretty colors they have? I've never seen such waves as there are on Mermaid Island."

Bonnie shrugged. She'd been wrapped up in her own troubles and really hadn't paid any attention to the water. In fact, she didn't intend to have anything do with the water or the beach, no matter how beautiful they were. Shopping was more her style. Tomorrow she would go look for interesting little gift shops–after the library, of course.

As Bonnie turned to put the computer away, her mother continued speaking to herself in a dreamy sort of voice.

"The waves look as if they've been touched with watercolors. Pinks and greens and yellows. Sort of like an abalone shell. When I was a child, I used to sit down on Yeoman's Beach to watch them. But that was many years ago. Now, where are the pillowcases?

Seems like I just saw them here. I want a pretty one for Bonnie's bed..."

Bonnie tiptoed away and set the computer on the desk in the corner room. Out the window, she glimpsed the waves rolling endlessly onto the beach and she frowned. They looked just like regular waves to her–turquoise and silver with foaming white tops.

Then she leaned closer to the window. Perhaps she did see a touch of pink. Yes, there was definitely something there. How very unusual, and very striking!

Bonnie looked down at the pearl around her neck, the translucent white swirled with touches of rose and azure. Like her pearl. The water had colors just like her pearl! With a last thoughtful glance out the window, Bonnie touched the gem with her fingertip, then returned to her room to finish her unpacking.

2

"Mom! I'm going to the library!" called Bonnie. She put her cereal bowl in the sink and rinsed it with hot water.

Her mother was sitting in the tiny corner room, her blonde hair mussed and her fingers flying over the keyboard of her laptop computer. Bonnie stuck her head in the door.

"Mom," she said again, and then "Mom!" more loudly.

Her mother looked up from the computer.

"Bonnie!" she said, her face breaking into a smile. "I didn't know you were up! Come see what I've done."

Bonnie looked over her mother's shoulder at the neat rows of figures and lists of plants identified with common and scientific names.

"What are you doing?" she asked.

"I'm organizing these flowers into a database," her mother answered, squinting at the screen. "I'm going to try to see if I can...now why did I put that there? That doesn't belong there."

A couple of keystrokes and the columns had reorganized themselves, although what had changed Bonnie couldn't tell.

"I shouldn't have put that there either," her mother continued, gazing intently at the screen. "I must be getting absent minded. It's the island and the water. I like to watch out the window too much. I must remind Bonnie to go to Yeoman's Beach. Bettina VanGelderen says it's still nearly exactly the same as it was when we were children."

"Mom," said Bonnie gently, and her mother looked up at her, startled.

"Oh! I'd forgotten you were there for a moment. This database has me all distracted. What is it, sweetheart?"

"I'm going to the library," said Bonnie. "They may have some of those Jane Forrester mysteries I like, and I want to see if they have any videos for loan."

"Good idea," said her mother. "Have a good time. Shall we barbecue tonight?"

Bonnie grinned. "I'd like that. See you later!"

She gave her mother a kiss on the cheek and headed for the front door. As she swung her backpack

14

over her shoulder, she caught a glimpse of herself in the mirror and frowned at her reflection.

Brown hair, brown eyes and a splatter of freckles across her nose. Why couldn't she have her mother's pixie-like build and corn silk hair? Instead, Bonnie was tall and her hair was thick and long, waving nearly to the middle of her back, the color of autumn oak leaves.

It would be nice if her hair were an interesting color, Bonnie thought. Like that girl she'd seen by the library. Red hair...now that would be different! She imagined herself transformed, with auburn hair flowing around sparkling green eyes. Then she shook her head at herself. Grabbing a rubber band off the counter, she tied her hair back in a ponytail and pushed out the screen door.

The morning was crisp and cool, and Bonnie hurried up the street, nodding at an elderly couple walking a little spotted dog.

"Morning," they said, and Bonnie murmured, "morning..."

They must be her neighbors, she thought. She'd heard a dog barking the evening before. Having a dog would be nice. A little dog to take around the island with her so she had a friend. She sighed gently. Ah–there was the library. Bonnie pushed open the glass door and walked inside.

The library was dark and quiet, with soft reading lights arranged around big comfortable chairs, and wood paneled rows of bookshelves. There were a few patrons browsing in the magazine section and flipping through paperbacks, and Bonnie gave a contented sigh. Libraries could be fun or they could be boring. This one felt just right.

She headed straight to the mystery section and picked up a Jane Forrester novel she hadn't read. The Wild Water Mystery. That was the perfect title for an island-dweller, even a temporary one, Bonnie decided.

She was just about to tuck it under her arm when she caught a movement out of the corner of her eye. To her astonishment, she saw the red-haired girl she'd spied the day before approaching her, a tentative smile on her face.

Bonnie smiled back and the girl cocked her head to see the title of the book Bonnie was holding, her face breaking into a broad grin. To Bonnie's surprise, she saw a pair of laughing green eyes, just like the ones she'd imagined in the mirror that morning.

"The Wild Water Mystery. That's a really good one," said the girl. "I've read it about three times. How about you?"

"I haven't read it before," replied Bonnie. "It was always checked out at home. I thought it was a good book to read while I'm staying here this summer, though."

"I figured you were a summer visitor," said the girl, and held out a tanned hand. "I'm Bobbie VanGelderen. I live on the north side of the village."

Bonnie shook her hand. "My name is Bonnie Campbell, and I'm living in a cottage on the south side. My mother has a friend here named Bettina VanGelderen. Is that your mom?"

"My aunt," answered Bobbie. "They live next door to us. I guess there have been VanGelderens on Mermaid Island as long as anyone can remember, and there are several families. I live here year-round."

"Our names are a lot alike," commented Bonnie, and Bobbie broke into a peal of laughter that made a woman reading an art magazine glance over at them and frown.

Bobbie held her finger up to her lips and giggled, this time more softly.

"My real name is Ninaleen," she said. "I'm named after my grandmother. But my dad always thought Ninaleen sounded like some sort of a virus, and he began to call me Bobbie."

Bonnie thought privately that Ninaleen was a very beautiful name, but she didn't comment.

Instead, she whispered, "Do you come to the library often?"

"Oh yes, a lot," answered Bobbie. She tossed back a strand of her red hair. "Want to check out your book and go for a frollop? I'll tell you more about the island."

Wondering what a frollop was, Bonnie went to the counter and filled out a library card. Then she tucked the book into her backpack and followed Bobbie outside.

3

Bonnie and Bobbie strolled up the street, Bonnie looking curiously into the shop windows. She paused at a poster with big red letters.

"VILLAGE COUNCIL MEETING AUGUST 3," it read. "Yeoman's Beach development under discussion."

Bobbie grimaced at the sign. "Someone's always putting in new houses here," she said. "I can understand why people want to live on Mermaid Island, but it would wreck the environment to build on the beach."

Bobbie's auburn brows were drawn down over her eyes in a troubled frown, and Bonnie nodded sympathetically. Bonnie wondered if her mother knew about the building plan. She had mentioned Yeoman's

Beach just that morning. It seemed to have a special place in her heart.

"Well, let's go," said Bobbie finally, and they continued on down the sidewalk.

Bobbie stopped at a tiny shop with a bright yellow door. "The Frollop Shop" the storefront said.

"What's a frollop?" Bonnie asked curiously, and Bobbie grinned.

"A frollop is a frozen pop with a dollop of ice cream. Sort of like a soda, but Mr. Davis says it's got some other secret ingredients. He invented frollops, so he should know. It's his very secret recipe!"

"How many are there in your family?" Bonnie asked, as the two entered the store.

"Fifteen VanGelderens live on Mermaid Island," answered Bobbie. She slid onto a bar stool and patted the seat next to her for Bonnie to sit down. "My family, plus my aunt and uncle's family, my grandparents, and my great uncle."

"Do you have brothers and sisters?" asked Bonnie.

"Nope. Just me," said Bobbie. "But there are seven kids in my aunt and uncle's family, and since they live next door it's kind of like having a lot of brothers and sisters, only I can get away to my own house if I want some privacy. My cousins are always fighting over who gets to use the computer, and they all have to share rooms."

"I'm an only child, too," said Bonnie. "And my dad doesn't live with us. It's just my mom and me."

The two girls sat silently for a few minutes, reading through the menu and swinging their legs under the stools. Bonnie finally selected a peach frollop, and Bobbie had grape.

"Peach is one of my favorites," commented Bobbie, "but I like to keep a variety and I haven't had grape for a while. You'll have to try all the flavors. It's fun to have someone new to share frollops with."

Bonnie smiled at her, and thought with surprise, "And I thought I wouldn't have any friends on Mermaid Island!"

Bobbie reached across the counter and picked up a movie magazine.

"Gregor McNaughton!" she exclaimed, looking at the cover. "He is so great. Did you see 'My Father's Bride?' That was my favorite movie!"

"I liked 'Thirty Candles' best," answered Bonnie, "but 'My Father's Bride' was good, too."

Bobbie looked down at her frollop and then grinned. "I know a secret about Mermaid Island," she said. "Want to hear?"

"What sort of secret?" Bonnie asked cautiously. "Don't tell me if no one is supposed to know."

Bobbie giggled. "Well, Gregor McNaughton doesn't want anyone to know, but everyone here knows anyway. Secrets are hard to keep on this island. Come on, Bonnie! It's a fun secret."

"Okay," said Bonnie. "What is it?"

"Gregor McNaughton has a home here!" said Bobbie in a loud whisper. "It's out near Yeoman's, and it's just like a castle! He owns a ton of land and it's all fenced in to keep people away. He comes and goes by helicopter!"

"Really?!" said Bonnie, agog. "Gregor McNaughton, the movie star, has a home on Mermaid Island?"

"Really," said Bobbie, with the satisfied air of someone having just relayed a critically important piece of information. "I've peeked in his front gate lots of times. You can see the house, but just barely." Bobbie nodded wisely into her frollop.

"Wow," said Bonnie. "There sure is more to Mermaid Island than meets the eye."

"What do you mean?" asked Bobbie, glancing up.

"I just mean that there's a movie star living here, that's all," said Bonnie quickly, feeling rather guilty. She didn't want Bobbie to know how low her expectations of life on Mermaid Island had been. It was Bobbie's home, after all.

Bobbie smiled at her. "You probably don't think there's much to do here, do you?" Without waiting for

Bonnie to answer, Bobbie went on. "Well, it's up to me, then! Get ready for the summer of a lifetime."

Bonnie stared at her in surprise. "How did you know?" she asked.

Bobbie nodded in a knowing way and slurped up the last of her frollop with a burble that echoed through the store. Mr. Davis looked over at her indulgently.

"Lots of mainlanders think that Mermaid Island is just a big retirement village," she said. She looked up at Bonnie, her green eyes alight with mischief. "But I know better. I'll take it as a personal challenge to change your mind."

"Okay," answered Bonnie. "It's a deal!"

4

"Come look at this," shouted Bobbie from off in the woods, and Bonnie looked suspiciously at the rattling brush.

"Where are you?" she called. "And what are you doing?"

"Just come here!" came the answer, and Bonnie frowned.

So far Bobbie had dragged her into a creek, through a patch of raspberry bushes and across a field where Bonnie was nearly sure she saw poison ivy. She took a few tentative steps in Bobbie's direction and then glanced around, looking for anything that might be carnivorous or otherwise dangerous to a city girl with little knowledge of the woods. All she saw were ferns and a fallen tree, a few rocks and some greenish moss.

How could her mother tramp around in here all day, making notes, photographing plants and digging in the underbrush, Bonnie wondered? Just last night she had told Bonnie a long story about a little plant she had nearly missed seeing, but for a stray beam of sunlight that had suddenly shown her just where it was.

Her mother had been pacing back and forth in the living room, gesturing and laughing, her tiny feet encased in their heavy hiking boots and a smudge of black dirt on her left cheek. She looked as happy as Bonnie had ever seen her. The thought of it made Bonnie smile. She took a deep breath and plunged into the trees after her friend.

She found Bobbie kneeling under a bush, pointing at something growing near an old stump. Bonnie squinted in the direction of Bobbie's finger and saw three yellowish-orange mushrooms sprouting on thread-thin stems out of the rotting wood. Around them, moss frothed in rounded splashes, and a few red berries grew on some small, waxy-leafed plants.

"Isn't that cute?" said Bobbie, her face glowing. "Doesn't it look like an elves' palace?"

Bonnie inspected the stump, sat carefully down, and brushed off her ankles.

"Yes, it is cute," she said. "I can imagine little people living there."

She looked up at the blue sky, barely visible through the dense branches overhead. It must be mid-afternoon by now. Her stomach growled.

She had tried to act cheerful and interested as Bobbie led her on the tour of the forest, but apparently it hadn't fooled her, because Bobbie said, "Oh well, I can tell the forest isn't your thing. But I won't give up! I know I can make you love Mermaid Island just as I do."

"It really is beautiful," answered Bonnie guiltily. "It's just that I'm not really used to a lot of hiking around. I'm hungry, too. Mind if we head back?"

"Want to go over to Yeoman's and walk down the beach for a few minutes before we go?" asked Bobbie cheerfully, jumping to her feet and apparently unbothered that their venture into the woods hadn't been successful.

"Yes, let's do that," said Bonnie eagerly. "My mom loves it there and she wanted me to visit. Besides, I like looking at the waves. They're such beautiful colors."

Bobbie glanced at her but said nothing, and the two started down a path through the trees toward the sound of the water. For a while they walked in silence. Then Bobbie spoke, her brow furrowed.

"It's interesting to hear you say that about the waves," she said. "I've heard other people mention the colors, too, but I don't notice anything unusual. My cousin Moonie says she sees pink and gold all the time, but I've always thought she was making it up."

"You have a cousin named Moonie?" asked Bonnie.

"Her name is really Mona," said Bobbie, "but we all call her Moonie."

"Does anyone in your family go by their real name?" asked Bonnie jokingly, and Bobbie laughed.

"Well, Carlotta Anastasia does," she answered, but just when Bonnie started to demand who Carlotta Anastasia was, Bobbie halted abruptly and Bonnie almost ran into her.

"Bonnie, tell me honestly. Do you see pink and gold in the waves?"

Bonnie hesitated. Bobbie sounded envious and perhaps a little hurt.

"Well, there's a lot of sunshine here," Bonnie said cautiously. "Where we live it's foggy a lot and of course there's no water. I expect it's just a trick of the light. After all," she added kindly, "if you, a Mermaid Island native, have never seen anything, then I'm probably imagining it."

Bobbie looked slightly mollified and began to walk again, her red hair bobbing along in its tight braid. "Other people think they see colors besides Moonie, though. Moonie says it's something special about Mermaid Island, but she's always dreaming about stuff. That's why we call her Moonie."

Just then, the two girls broke out of the trees into a short strip of knee-high grass. Beyond it, the surf pounded the beach and the sun glinted on shining sand. Water spilled over rocks just off the shoreline and bubbled gurgling into several small pools where driftwood sat in elaborate, curled sculptures carved by the gusting winds. The beach was deserted as far as Bonnie could see in either direction. She gasped.

5

"Yeoman's Beach," announced Bobbie, like a guide on a tour bus.

She turned to her friend and laughed at the astounded expression on Bonnie's face. "Isn't it just like something out of a picture book?"

"Oh yes!" Bonnie agreed, but what had taken her breath away was the sight of the water.

The colors! Waves tipped with maroon and aqua and lavender and copper danced and flashed in the bright sunshine. The hues were as deep and as rich as if they'd been touched on with a giant's paintbrush, curling and swirling and blending with the deep blue water like a sunset dropped out of the sky.

She opened her mouth and then closed it, making Bobbie burst into delighted laughter .

"I've figured it out!" she exclaimed, "and it was so easy! Yeoman's Beach is how you'll fall in love with Mermaid Island." She grinned. "That was hardly even a challenge!"

Bonnie sank down with a sigh, lifting up handfuls of the warm sand and letting the sparkling crystals slide through her fingers.

"Is this all public land?" she asked at last. "Where are all the day visitors and boaters?"

"Most people use the beach by the ferry landing," said Bobbie. "That's where the bait stores and souvenir shops and restaurants are."

"It seems like people would want to come down here where it's more private. It's so beautiful!" breathed Bonnie, looking out at the long stretch of empty sand and the glittering water. "It's the most beautiful place I've ever seen!"

Bobbie was right, it looked like something out of a picture book. Bonnie had never known places like this really existed.

"Maybe they go to the other beaches because Yeoman's is completely undeveloped," Bobbie suggested. "There are houses north of here and on the east side too, but this part of the island is a natural area. There isn't any building allowed."

"But the sign in town..." Bonnie began, and Bobbie nodded.

That's what the Village Council meeting is all about," she said soberly. "Someone is trying to build summer homes here or something."

Bonnie jumped to her feet. "They can't do that, Bobbie! Look at this place! Look at the sand and the trees and the sky. Look at the waves, the col…" Bonnie stopped herself. "Look at the driftwood!"

Bobbie looked at Bonnie curiously, but didn't comment, so Bonnie hurried on, "Oh, I hope the Village Council can do something. I know there is nowhere like this anywhere else on earth!"

Bobbie frowned. "A lot of people here on the island are opposed to building on Yeoman's," she replied. "There are other places to build that wouldn't destroy the natural habitat."

Bonnie nodded in agreement. She stood dreamily, staring out at the swirling water, then caught sight of something odd out of the corner of her eye and jumped violently.

"What was that?!" she exclaimed shrilly.

Out in the water, a silvery shape had flashed across the waves. For a moment, Bonnie stared after it, open mouthed, trying to decide what she had seen. It was gone so quickly she couldn't be sure, but her mind formed the image of a hand and part of a slender white arm. The arm was draped in a long drift of lacy weed tipped in pinks and yellows and blues and greens.

Fingers with glinting silver nails had been grasping the peaks of the waves as they sped toward shore, and the waves' white caps looked like the long, flowing hair of a woman.

Bonnie's heart was hammering so hard that she pressed one fist against her chest. Beneath her clenched fingers, she could feel her grandmother's pearl, smooth and round against her skin. Was it warmer suddenly, or was it her imagination? The sound of Bobbie's calling crept into her consciousness, and she turned toward her alarmed friend.

"Bonnie! Bonnie!" cried Bobbie. "What did you see? What did you SEE?!"

Bobbie was staring with frightened eyes toward the water.

Now that a few moments had passed, Bonnie felt her heartbeat slowing and she took a deep breath. Loosening her fingers from the pearl, she smiled shakily at Bobbie.

"It's all right," she murmured, and Bobbie stared at her in confusion.

Bobbie's face was as white as the foaming water, and some of her red hair had come loose from her braid. It blew nearly straight up in the stiff wind, looking crazily like a big red horn.

"What did you see?" Bobbie gasped again, "What was it?"

"I don't know," said Bonnie. She felt very tired suddenly, and sluggish, as if she had just awakened from a deep sleep. "I saw someone. Or at least I thought I did. Maybe someone swimming or a big fish or something. It was under the waves."

She giggled suddenly. "Bobbie, your hair..."

But Bobbie didn't seem amused. "If that's supposed to be a joke, it isn't very funny. You really scared me!" Her eyes narrowed. "And what about my hair? What's wrong with it?" she demanded.

Bobbie looked so offended that Bonnie hastened to reassure her.

"I'm sorry if I scared you. I did think I saw something," she replied. "It looked like a hand or an arm, something in the water."

"But why were you just standing there?" Bobbie asked. "You looked like you were about to faint! I didn't know what to do!"

"Oh, Bobbie, I'm sorry!" Bonnie apologized. "I was scared myself for a minute. Then I felt weird...like I couldn't move or something. I really thought I saw something in the water, though. Honestly!"

Bobbie looked suspiciously into Bonnie's brown eyes and then said, relenting, "Well, what do you think it was?"

Bonnie looked over her shoulder. The water looked normal. The colors were nearly gone. Only a hint of rose on the tips of the tallest waves remained, and even that was fading. Did she have an hallucination or something? What had gotten into her?

She stared at Bobbie in consternation, and Bobbie forgave her. "It's all right," she said. "I just don't like to be scared, and, well...never mind Let's just forget it, okay?"

"Okay," said Bonnie, casting a last glance at the waves.

It must have been a log or something, she thought firmly, but her fingers crept up and touched her grandmother's pearl.

6

By late that afternoon, Bonnie and Bobbie had decided the whole incident was so funny that they could hardly talk about it without going into hysterics. They sat together in folding chairs on Bonnie's lawn, sipping frollops and laughing until Bonnie had the hiccups.

"…and your hair, Bobbie," howled Bonnie, "You looked like you'd seen a ghost."

"Ooooh whooo, I am the ghost of the sailor Peg Leg Sam. I am going to eat your frollop," chortled Bobbie.

"Who's a ghost?" said Bonnie's mother, looking out the screen door. "Hi Bobbie!"

"Mom! You're home," Bonnie jumped up. "We've been exploring, and I went to Yeoman's today. Wait 'til you hear what happened to us…"

"It must have been something good, because you have the hiccups," said Bonnie's mother, and grinned at Bobbie. "Whenever she's been giggling a lot she gets the hiccups."

"It was so funny! Listen, mom—we were standing on the beach and I was looking out at the waves," Bonnie glanced at Bobbie. She'd decided not to mention the colors anymore. It was too spooky, and besides it made Bobbie unhappy. "And suddenly I thought I saw something in the water. It was sort of like an ice sculpture, or maybe a water balloon."

"A water balloon?" shrieked Bobbie. "The ghost of the Mermaid Island water balloon!"

"No, Bobbie, wait! I'm trying to explain…"

But Bobbie was laughing so hard that she nearly tipped her chair over backwards, and by the time Bonnie and her mother had rescued her the two of them had also begun to laugh helplessly.

"I know," Bonnie finally gasped. "We'll call it the Case of the Ominous Water Balloon."

"Sounds good to me," said Bobbie, whose face was pink and the rest of her hair had come out of its braid.

Bonnie's mother grinned at them. "You are like two peas in a pod, you know that? Bobbie, I'm so glad you made friends with my daughter." She ruffled Bonnie's hair and then went to stow her computer and briefcase in the corner room.

"I'd better go on home," said Bobbie, slurping the last of her frollop. "Want to come over tomorrow and meet my family?"

"Sure," answered Bonnie, and walked Bobbie to the door.

She was relieved that Bobbie wasn't angry anymore, but she couldn't stop thinking about what had happened that day. Something about it nagged at her, and she felt vaguely uneasy.

Later that evening, Bonnie sat with her mother on the back lawn licking mustard from her hamburger off her fingers and staring out at the waves.

"Mermaid Island has a secret," she commented.

Her mother glanced at her. "I'm sure it has plenty," she answered mildly.

"Bobbie told me about it," continued Bonnie. "It isn't exactly a secret, though. I think pretty much everyone who lives here knows it." She wiped the rest of the mustard on her napkin and wadded it up next to her plate. "Here it is. Gregor McNaughton has a house on the island! It's over by Yeoman's. Bobbie said she's seen it through the gate and it's as big as a palace!"

"Gregor McNaughton? Isn't he a movie star?" asked Bonnie's mom.

"Of course he's a movie star, mom!" exclaimed Bonnie. "He's about the most famous person there is. Don't you remember 'Thirty Candles?'"

"Did I see that?" her mother answered vaguely. "Yes, I guess I did…"

Bonnie bounded to her feet. "It was the one where he went on the motorcycle trip and helped the woman with the opal ring. How can you have forgotten it? It was the best movie ever!"

Caro Campbell smiled at her daughter. "I'm sort of teasing you. Yes, I do remember it. So McNaughton has a house on Mermaid Island? I didn't know there were any celebrity homes here."

"Bobbie offered to take me over for a peek," ventured Bonnie. "Think it would hurt anything?"

"So long as you stay on the public road, it should be okay," said her mother. "But don't go on his land, and don't harass him or anything."

"We won't," Bonnie assured her. "And do you know what?" she added. "Someone's trying to develop Yeoman's. I saw a sign about it on the street by the Library."

"Develop Yeoman's?!" Now her mother sounded alarmed. "Who is, and why?"

"I don't know," answered Bonnie, "But, there's a Village Council meeting to vote on it."

Bonnie would have gone on speaking, but Caro Campbell was hurrying back toward the cottage, talking to herself.

"I've got to call Bettina VanGelderen. Would the council really consider turning that natural area into a development? There must be hundreds of endangered flowers in the woods there. I had hoped Bonnie could..."

Bonnie heard the door slam and her mother dialing the telephone. "Bettina! How are you? I just heard the most terrible news..."

Bonnie smiled. Her mother would do something to stop the development, she was sure of it. She could hear her mom's voice rising and falling as she talked to her friend on the phone, and Bonnie leaned her head back in her chair. She felt contented, tired and suddenly very sleepy.

As she watched the water ebb and flow through half-closed eyes, she saw colors begin to creep into the waves. They were very subtle at first, but grew in brightness until the waves were accented in gold and maroon and magenta, all swirling and fantastic against the darkening sky.

"There it is again," thought Bonnie lazily. "I wonder what makes the water do that?"

But she was too drowsy to be very curious and too snug in her comfortable chair to get excited. Instead, she watched the waves through her lashes and only blinked when a long silver-green tail, frosted with gold and copper, slid gently through the surf.

A slender white arm and a hand with silver-tipped nails closed cautiously over the crest of a long wave. Then an oval face appeared, framed in a cascade of silver hair. Sparkling glints of red and blue twisted and curled in the eddying water.

Rousing, Bonnie's eyes widened and she had just opened her mouth to call out in surprise when with a whirl and a shimmer the figure was gone, and nothing was left but the empty water. Bonnie's eyes slowly closed and she drifted into a deep slumber. Out in the waves, the colors faded slowly until nothing was left but a touch of pink, barely visible in the dying light of the evening.

7

"Moonie says Mr. Davis puts something in frollops that makes it so you can't stop eating them," announced Bobbie, gesturing at the door to the Frollop Shop.

"I wouldn't be surprised," said Bonnie, peering into the pink froth remaining at the bottom of her cup, "I don't think I've ever had anything so delicious!"

They were sitting on the bench outside the Frollop Shop on Main Street, swinging their legs and watching passersby.

"Good thing we finished these when we did," joked Bobbie. "If we took them to my house, my cousins would probably jump on us and steal them."

"How many frollops have we had since I got here?" grinned Bonnie. "I bet about five."

"I had more," laughed Bobbie. "I sneaked one when you had to go home one afternoon."

Bonnie laughed along with her, then stood up, brushing off her shorts.

"What flavor does Moonie like?" she asked.

"Usually pear," said Bobbie. "In fact, Mr. Davis introduced pear just for her. Everyone knows how much Moonie likes pears. And everyone likes Moonie," she added.

The two girls began walking down the road toward the north side of town and Bobbie's house. It was a hot, breezy day, but Bonnie didn't like the look of the western sky. There were storm clouds gathering along the horizon.

"Moonie's at my house, in fact," Bobbie went on. "She's using the computer, because Flip has been hogging theirs."

"Is Flip your cousin, too?" asked Bonnie.

"Yes," said Bobbie. "Well, his name is really Frank, but he goes by Flip."

"Of course," said Bonnie weakly. It was going to take her forever to figure out Bobbie's family's names. There were twice as many as you normally had to learn.

"Moonie likes to write stories," Bobbie went on. "She writes them all the time, and they're real good. She borrows our computer so she can get away from Flip."

Bonnie nodded. Sometimes being an only child was a lot easier.

"I think Carlotta Anastasia is over, too," added Bobbie. "You can meet her along with the rest of the family."

"Who is..." began Bonnie, but just then Bobbie pointed across the street.

"Look at that!" she shouted, and sprinted away.

Bonnie scrambled after her. Bobbie stopped in front of a sign tacked on the wall of the Town Hall.

"Rezoning Notice," it said, and Bobbie turned to Bonnie in fury. "Look at this!" she exclaimed. "It's the plan for the Yeoman's development. All those houses! And now a heliport?"

"A heliport?" quizzed Bonnie. "Isn't that a place where helicopters..."

"Where helicopters land, that's right!" answered Bobbie. She stomped her foot. "It'll drive away all the animals and totally wreck the beach! And why a heliport? Hardly anyone lives here except in the summer!"

"What about the Village Council? Won't they be able to stop it?" asked Bonnie.

"Good question," answered Bobbie grimly.

Bobbie and Bonnie stared at each other in consternation.

"Come on, Bonnie," said Bobbie. "Maybe my mom knows something about this."

In a few moments, the girls were walking up to the door of a small white house with blue shutters. There were marigolds tumbling out of containers on the porch and the windows were open toward the breeze. Bonnie could hear soft music drifting through the curtains.

"Moonie's definitely over," said Bobbie. "She loves music."

The door opened and a brown-haired woman with blue jeans and a straw hat started out. She was carrying a bag of wood chips and a bucket.

"Hi Bobbie! I was just going to put in the rest of those marigolds before it rains," said the woman, then, "Oh hello!" as she spied Bonnie.

"Hello," said Bonnie politely, and Bobbie introduced Bonnie to her mother.

"You may call me Polly," said Mrs. VanGelderen. "Everyone does."

Just then there was a loud SNORT! and a crunch from somewhere within the house, and Polly looked over her shoulder.

"Carlotta Anastasia!" she called. "Get out of the kitchen!"

Bonnie looked at Bobbie in confusion. "What was that?" she asked.

"Oh, that was Carlotta Anastasia," said Bobbie offhandedly. "She's always into some sort of mischief."

"Who is..." tried Bonnie once again, but again she was interrupted.

"Moonie!" called Polly. "Go get Carlotta Anastasia! Sounds like she's getting into something."

"Carlotta Anastasia!" came a singsong voice from behind Polly, and over Polly's shoulder Bonnie saw a tallish girl with light brown hair and sparkling hazel eyes stride into the room.

Behind her bounced the oddest looking little dog Bonnie had ever seen. She was tan with a black face and a curly tail, and her nose was flat and shiny below two round black eyes. Her body was fat and sturdy, and her little pink tongue lolled as she puffed along behind the girl.

"Hi," said the girl softly, and Bobbie introduced her cousin.

"This is Moonie," she said. "And that," she pointed at the little dog, "is Carlotta Anastasia."

"Oh," answered Bonnie, staring. "What kind of a dog is Carlotta Anastasia?"

"She's a pug," said Moonie merrily, and reached down to pick up the little animal. "Isn't she the cutest?"

Carlotta Anastasia gazed at Bonnie and snorted quietly through her flat black nose. Her small wrinkled forehead looked worried.

Bonnie grinned at her. "Carlotta Anastasia, I'm happy to meet you!" she said.

At that, Carlotta Anastasia, her curly tail wagging madly, wriggled out of Moonie's arms and sat down on Bonnie's foot, panting happily.

Polly had wandered off toward the garden and Bobbie ran after her, explaining about the sign they'd seen in town. Moonie remained standing with Bonnie, listening from a distance. Her mouth tightened when she heard Bobbie mention the heliport.

"They just can't do that to Yeoman's Beach," she exclaimed. "This is terrible!"

"I think so, too," said Bonnie, her voice trailing off.

She thought back to the long stretch of glittering sand, the thick stands of trees bending their green branches toward the beach, and the water...always that water. It looked as if it had been touched with all the colors of the rainbow.

Bonnie looked up suddenly and found Moonie watching her closely.

"Er," she said. Had she been rude? For a moment, her mind had drifted back to the beach and strange object she'd seen in the water. She was sure it wasn't a log, but if not, what was it? And then she'd had the oddest dream while dozing in her chair. The colors had come again, and then she'd seen...what?

Bobbie strode back up to them, interrupting Bonnie's reverie. "Mom didn't know about the rezoning, but she's going to call her friends," she said. "They're going to try to figure out what's going on."

Bonnie and Moonie exchanged glances and Bonnie smiled. There was something about Moonie. Bonnie liked her instantly, and Bobbie had said Moonie saw the colors in the water. Maybe someday Bonnie could ask her about them.

What made them, and why were they sometimes nearly invisible and sometimes so brilliant?

Moonie pulled a small silver object out of her pocket, displaying it for Bonnie and Bobbie.

"I got a new camera," she said. "It takes instant photos, see? The pictures are really great, too. Bonnie, go stand over there by Bobbie. I'll take your picture!"

Moonie snapped the photo and then pulled a strip of paper out of the back of the camera. On it, Bonnie could see an image start to emerge of her and Bobbie standing in front of Polly's marigolds.

"Oh!" she said, delighted. "Look how clear it is! May I have it?" she asked eagerly. "It would be a great souvenir!"

"Sure," answered Moonie, and handed it to Bonnie. Bonnie thanked her and slipped it into her pocket.

A low rumble of thunder sounded in the distance and Bobbie glanced up at the threatening sky.

"Let's go inside 'til the rain passes," she said. "I can show you my room. Come on Moonie," she added, "and bring Carlotta Anastasia!"

8

When the rain stopped, Bonnie started home, taking the beach path rather than walking through the village. Across the water, angry clouds boiled as the storm moved away from the island.

The air was still heavy and rather sullen, but the waves were quiet and their lapping against the sand sounded soothing and musical. Bonnie sighed gently. How different her summer had turned out to be than what she had feared. The days were flying by so quickly it made her head spin.

In the distance, she could see the lights from their cottage burning in the gentle twilight. Her mother had held dinner while Bonnie waited out the rain at Bobbie's house. Perhaps they would eat out in the back yard again.

Suddenly Bonnie felt a sense of warmth and drowsiness creep over her and she stopped walking, turning to gaze curiously out at the horizon. To her surprise, tinges of magenta and copper had begun to color the tips of the tossing waves and an aquamarine pool was spreading steadily out over the water just off the shoreline.

She closed her hand over the pearl and dug her toes in the sand, swaying slightly and watching the fantastic colors deepen. It was happening again! Bonnie wanted to run, but somehow her body felt heavy and awkward and her brain had stopped working properly. Was she sick? She shook her head, fighting to stay alert.

The aquamarine began to grow even bluer, gathering to nearly indigo in the center. Bonnie heart was pounding in her chest despite the odd sluggishness, and she was torn between fright and wonder. Her whole consciousness felt as if it was focused on those growing, swirling colors. What was going to happen? What should she do?

"Bonnie," her mother's voice called from the distance, and Bonnie jumped. "What are you doing out there?"

Caro Campbell was walking quickly across the wet sand, watching Bonnie inquiringly. Her short blonde hair was tousled and her jacket flapped in the wind.

"Oh!" Bonnie exclaimed. She gave herself a shake as her mother walked up to her. "I was on my way home," Bonnie answered, "but I stopped to watch the water for a minute."

She glanced over her shoulder, but the waves suddenly looked perfectly normal. A slight mist hovered just above the crests, but the dazzling colors were gone. Whatever had been happening had stopped.

"I made a noodle casserole. It just came out of the oven," said her mother. "Better come on home before it gets cold."

"Okay," said Bonnie. She couldn't resist looking out at the water again, and her mother followed her gaze.

She smiled. "The waves are a pretty color tonight, aren't they?" she commented. "Must be the rain and the sunset."

"Pinkish? Is that how they look to you sometimes?" asked Bonnie. "With copper or silver, and blues and greens, and...well, all sorts of colors?"

"I've often wished I could paint it," sighed her mother, "but of course I've never been able to paint a thing. And besides, it's too subtle to capture. It's more like a feeling than something you can see."

Bonnie glanced at the water again. What she had seen wasn't subtle at all, but brilliant swirls of gleaming colors that lit up the water.

Thinking very hard, Bonnie followed her mother the rest of the way up the beach and into their cabin.

After dinner, while Bonnie cleared the table and packed her mother's lunch for the next day, Caro Campbell sat at the kitchen table and stared at the darkened windows, a frown gathering on her brows.

"What's the matter, mom?" asked Bonnie.

"I've been talking to Bettina VanGelderen and some other folks in town," she answered, "about the problem with Yeoman's and the building project."

Her mother was drinking a cup of tea and she stopped to take a sip.

"No one can figure out why a company would want to put in a heliport, and the company that has put in the rezoning request won't tell where the idea came from. They will only say that it's a reasonable way of bringing people over from the mainland."

"But why out there?" she mused. "Why on Yeoman's? It's so remote, and even if they do build houses they don't need a helicopter to get to them. I should call over to the mainland and see if the ferry company can tell me if someone's planning to open a business that sells helicopter rides for tourists. Yes! I bet that's it!"

Her mother bounded to her feet. "Tomorrow before I leave for the field, I'm going to get to the bottom of this. Someone must have some answers!"

Bonnie smiled at her. It was comforting to know her mother was working on the problem. She was determined to save Yeoman's Beach, and when her mother set her mind on something she was just about unstoppable.

Later, up in her room, Bonnie sat on her bed and thought for a long time, fingering the pearl around her neck. When she had been out on the beach, it hadn't been just the colors. She had sensed something else.

There had been someone *there.* Someone out in the water. She was certain of it.

Finally, she walked to her dresser and opened her jewelry box. Inside, a dozen glass beads in all the colors of the rainbow lay nestled in the black velvet. She had bought them thinking she might make them into jewelry someday, but now she had a better use for them.

Sorting them carefully, she selected two and tucked them in the pocket of her shorts. Quietly, she walked to the door and went outside into the night. Behind her she could hear her mother on the phone with someone, and she sounded agitated.

Bonnie heard her say, "Well we can fight, even if we're a small community," and Bonnie smiled to herself.

Bonnie strode down to the beach and stood on the sand close to the water, her eyes searching the horizon. The moon had come up. It shone brightly among the shifting clouds and here and there she could see the foaming white cap of a wave as it rolled toward the shore.

Walking quickly along the sand, Bonnie spied a log jutting out into the water, its upended roots like a silky gray fan where the wind and the waves had scoured them.

Balancing her weight carefully, she walked out onto the makeshift bridge. Then, crouching down, she tucked the beads into a hollow between two thick branches.

Back on the beach, she stood gazing out into the water for several moments, watching and waiting.

"I brought you a gift," she whispered, and not knowing whether to feel frightened or silly, she hurried back to the cabin.

Inside, she found herself more inclined to feel silly and she threw her sneakers under the bed with more force than was necessary. Then she changed out of her shorts and tumbled into bed, feeling annoyed with herself.

"I must be going crazy," she thought. "It's the storm, or my imagination running away with me. I didn't see a face. How could there be anyone out in the water?"

She punched her pillow grumpily and turned on her side. In the morning she would fetch her beads back and forget about her ridiculous "gift."

Outside, around the log where Bonnie had left the glass beads, the waves began to shimmer pink and copper, and a deep indigo pool spread slowly over the quiet water.

9

The next morning when Bonnie scampered down to the log to get the beads, she found herself staring open-mouthed at the spot where she'd left them. They were gone.

She gazed out into the water, but there was nothing and no one there. The beach stretched quiet and deserted, the waves lost in their endless dance over the sand under a sunny blue sky.

Thinking very hard, Bonnie returned slowly home, pausing every now and then to look back at the water.

An idea was beginning to form in her mind. It was a strange, fantastic idea, but what other explanation was there for what she'd seen, and for the disappearance of her glass beads? She'd offered them as a gift, and her gift had been accepted.

Bonnie's heart had begun to pound, and she was smiling excitedly as she pushed open the screen door to the cottage.

She found her mother inside, packing her backpack and the laptop computer, hunting for the car keys and throwing bottles of lemonade into the cooler. Today she was going to the far side of the island, deep into the woods to continue her plant survey, and she intended to be gone the whole day.

"What are you going to do today, Bonnie?" she asked.

"What?" answered Bonnie, who was still deep in thought. Then she said slowly, "I think I'm going to stay here today."

She put her cereal bowl on the table and pulled out a cup for some orange juice. "Bobbie's gone with some school friends to the mainland, and I'm just going to read and relax and consider things."

"Consider things? Sounds very mysterious! Want to come with me to the woods instead?" offered her mother.

Bonnie grinned. "Thanks for the offer, but no. I'm not sure I'm ready to be in the woods all day. I'd rather stay by the beach."

"I like the woods," her mother responded, putting a baseball cap on her head and balancing her sunglasses on her nose. "It's quiet and I can think clearly while I'm there. Besides, my research is coming along great. You can't believe the number of plants I've found!"

With that, her tiny mother shouldered the heavy pack, tossed the car keys into her pocket and headed for the door, humming to herself.

"Bye!" she called to Bonnie, and Bonnie waved.

After breakfast, Bonnie read a Jane Forrester book for a while, then headed down to the beach, finding a spot in the shade to watch the water. The waves looked nearly regular today. There were no colors to speak of and the steady breeze blowing from the north was crisp and cool. The rain had cleared the air.

"Where are you?" Bonnie whispered to the tossing waves. "Did you like the present I left you?"

No one answered, and Bonnie got to her feet. Whatever was happening was somehow connected to the colors in the water. But other people saw the colors, didn't they? Maybe not so brightly as Bonnie did, but they saw at least something. Year-round Mermaid Island dwellers might know if there was anything really peculiar in the water.

Nodding to herself, Bonnie went back to the cabin, changed her clothes and walked into the village to visit the library. If there was any information to be found about unusual legends of Mermaid Island, that's where she would find it.

To her surprise, sitting on the bench in front of the library and reading a paperback book was Moonie.

Moonie looked up at Bonnie's approach and smiled. "Hi Bonnie!"

"Hi!" Bonnie answered "What are you reading?"

Moonie showed her. It was a book about corals.

"I'd like to be an oceanographer someday," explained Moonie. "Or maybe a marine biologist. Are you going in the library?"

"Yes," replied Bonnie. "I was hoping to get some history on Mermaid Island."

"Oh, they've got quite a lot of stuff," responded Moonie. "I'll go with you," she volunteered.

Inside, Moonie led her to the local history section and Bonnie picked up a thin volume called Mermaid Island: A Retrospective.

"The librarian, Mr. Conner, wrote that," offered Moonie. "He knows a lot about the island."

"Great," said Bonnie. "Do you want to go and read somewhere?" she asked. "It's a nice day to be outside."

"Sure," answered Moonie, and they started for the front door.

Moonie paused by the magazine rack. "Look," she said, and picked up the current issue of MovieNews. On the cover was a photo of Gregor McNaughton, flashing a huge smile with his gleaming white teeth.

Moonie grinned at Bonnie. "You know our island 'secret,' right?" she asked.

"You mean about Gregor McNaughton?" ventured Bonnie.

"I figured you did," answered Moonie, and laughed. "He's really a nut about his privacy, but everyone here knows he has a house on the island."

Bonnie didn't answer. She was beginning to suspect that Mermaid Island had an even bigger secret that perhaps no one knew except herself.

Moonie's head was bent over the magazine cover and Bonnie studied her profile. Bobbie had hinted that Moonie saw bright colors in the waves like Bonnie did. What would Moonie say if Bonnie asked her about what might be living in the water off Yeoman's beach?

Just then Moonie looked up, her hazel eyes sparkling, and the moment was lost. "It says here that Gregor McNaughton is about to begin shooting his next movie," she said. "It's in Italy."

"Really?" Bonnie glanced over her shoulder and read: "The famous actor is about to travel to Italy to begin shooting his next movie, 'The Baker Strategy.' He'll be teamed up with the leading lady from 'Thirty Candles,' Tina Carew, who is his latest love interest."

Bonnie made a face. "I'd hate to be an actress," she commented. "Or at least I'd hate how everyone always writes everything about you in magazines."

"That's why he tries to keep his house here so secret," said Moonie. "When you're a big star like that, it would be hard to find any time alone. He owns a ton of property around his house, and has a big wall. Have you seen it?"

"No," answered Bonnie. "Bobbie and I talked about going out there, but we haven't done it yet. I'd like to, though."

"You can look at his house from the road without hurting anything," said Moonie. "It isn't like you're trespassing on his property. I'll take you there sometime if you'd like," she offered.

"Maybe all three of us can go," said Bonnie.

"That would be fun," Moonie replied.

She put the magazine back on the shelf, and they walked outside. Moonie took a deep breath of the fresh breeze and smiled. "It sure is a beautiful day. Want to take our books and go read on the beach? We can bring Carlotta Anastasia so she can have some exercise."

"Sure," said Bonnie eagerly. Maybe she would have another chance to ask Moonie about the colors in the water!

On the way to pick up Carlotta Anastasia, they passed in front of the Frollop Shop.

"Want to?" said Moonie, gesturing at the bright yellow door.

"Why not?" answered Bonnie, laughing. "I haven't tried watermelon yet."

"Oh, it's wonderful," said Moonie, pushing open the shop door. "But you haven't lived 'til you've had pear!"

10

Sipping their frollops, Moonie and Bonnie strolled down Main Street, Carlotta Anastasia puffing along behind them. Moonie poured some of her frollop into the cup top and let Carlotta Anastasia lap it out. Bonnie giggled at the ice cream the little dog tried to lick off her flat nose.

As they neared the end of the street, a light blue sedan pulled over to the curb and a well-dressed man wearing a straw cowboy hat stepped out.

"Morning, Mr. Veenstra," said Moonie.

"Morning, Moonie VanGelderen," said the man, tipping his hat to Moonie and Bonnie.

"Mr. Veenstra is on the Village Council," said Moonie. "He's the chairman. Mr. Veenstra, this is Bonnie Campbell. She's here for the summer."

"Nice to meet you," said Bonnie politely.

Mr. Veenstra smiled at her, and Bonnie ventured, "What do you think about the Yeoman's Beach rezoning, Mr. Veenstra?"

He frowned at her. "The council has filed for all the paperwork, and we have correspondence from the developer under review."

He was looking rather pointedly toward the Town Hall, so Bonnie and Moonie thanked him and continued on their walk.

"Mr. Veenstra's pretty new on the island," said Moonie thoughtfully, "but so far he's been a good council chair."

"He didn't seem to want to talk about Yeoman's Beach," commented Bonnie.

"It's probably got the council just as angry as everyone else," speculated Moonie. "Maybe they're still trying to read everything."

"Probably," answered Bonnie. "Are your parents going to the meeting?"

"For sure," said Moonie firmly. "They wouldn't miss it for anything."

"We're going, too," said Bonnie. "I hope the whole village turns out."

"Oh, it will," answered Moonie. "No one's going to miss this meeting!"

Soon Bonnie and Moonie had left the village and entered the short stretch of forested road that led to Yeoman's Beach. Moonie unsnapped Carlotta Anastasia's leash and the little dog trotted off to root in the bushes for a few minutes before scampering after her mistress, snuffling loudly.

"Carlotta Anastasia is always snorting," pointed out Bonnie, when Carlotta Anastasia fell into step at Moonie's heels.

"All pugs do that," said Moonie, laughing, and Bonnie laughed along with her. "It's part of their charm."

When they reached Yeoman's Beach, they sat down in a lightly shaded spot and opened their books to read, Bonnie eagerly scanning through the table of contents of Mr. Conner's book to see if she could find any information on island legends. Surely if anyone had seen a mer...anything unusual in the water, it would be recorded in the island's history.

A pleasant hour slid past. Bonnie kicked her sandals off and curled her toes in the warm sand, then took her hair down from its rubber band so the wind could blow it back from her face. It really was a beautiful day, she thought idly. On a day like this, almost anything could happen.

Glancing up at the water, her eyes widened as she saw colors begin to spread across the waves. Here gold and ivory; there aqua and peach and bronze.

There it is again! Bonnie thought excitedly.

Hardly daring to breathe, she glanced over at Moonie, who was still reading quietly, her hazel eyes fixed on the printed page in front of her.

"Moonie!" said Bonnie urgently, and Moonie looked up from her book, her gaze curious but unalarmed.

Bonnie was starting to feel sleepy, and that strange sluggishness she'd felt before was creeping into her muscles. She struggled to keep her eyes open and to concentrate. How was it possible that Moonie could stay sitting so calmly next to her? Couldn't she tell what was going on?

Bonnie shook her head groggily, determined not to fall asleep. What was happening? Why did she keep having these spells of such tremendous sleepiness?

Before her bewildered eyes, she suddenly saw the water start to swirl and dance around a widening aqua pool. The colors became even more intense, and in the center of the pool, the waves diminished to tiny lapping ripples.

Then, to Bonnie's amazement, a young woman's face of the most startling beauty arose out of the water, framed by flowing silver hair, her skin a dazzling white. Eyes as green as emeralds gazed out from beneath lashes tipped with silver and jade.

Her pink lips were slightly parted, and her skin glittered faintly, as if it were sprinkled with diamond dust. Two hands tipped with oval silver nails lay lightly along the top of a tall wave arrested in its race to the shore. Her pale shoulders, rising just above the blue water, tapered from pearly white to emerald green, lapped with lightly scaled skin that glinted with copper and silver.

Time had stopped for Bonnie, and even the wind seemed to have been halted in its restless tossing of the leaves.

"I knew it," Bonnie's brain managed. "I knew it!" It was the face from her dream. The face in the waves.

The fantastic being in the water seemed to be gazing straight at Bonnie, her eyes gentle and curious beneath their strange and beautiful lashes. Bonnie could feel the pearl on its gold chain around her neck begin to glow and warm against her skin. With an effort, she moved her hand upward and clasped her fingers around the sphere.

"Grandma, if you only knew what was happening to me now," she thought hazily, and the mermaid's lips curved in a soft smile.

And then she was gone. Nothing remained in the water but a slight patch of mist, glimmering with pink and blue, and the tips of the waves touched with glinting copper, slowly fading to dull gold.

Bonnie blinked her eyes and then blinked again, trying desperately to clear her head. Despite everything that had happened, everything she had imagined, still she could hardly believe what she had seen. Even more fantastic was that Moonie, quietly turning a page in her book, appeared to have noticed nothing.

"Moonie!" Bonnie gasped, and Moonie turned her hazel gaze up from a photo of a salmon-colored coral formation.

"Moonie! I know you saw that. Tell me you did!" exclaimed Bonnie, and Moonie glanced out at the water.

"What?" she inquired. Then she said, "Oh, you mean the colors? It's strange, isn't it. Some sort of trick of the light, I imagine. They seem more brilliant to some people than to others."

"Yes, the colors, but also the..." Bonnie hesitated. Could Moonie sit there so calmly if she had seen what Bonnie had?

Bonnie stared suspiciously into her eyes, but saw nothing—not even the barest trace of a sign that Moonie was hiding anything. Perhaps she hadn't seen the face after all.

Bonnie sighed, and Moonie stretched and rose. "This sunshine is making me sleepy," she yawned. "Maybe we'd better go back. Besides, I need to watch my little brother while my mom goes shopping."

She brushed off the seat of her shorts and then extended a hand down to Bonnie to help her stand.

Bonnie struggled to her feet. Her knees felt weak and her skin tingly, as if she'd just come out of a cold shower.

She glanced around her. "Where's Carlotta Anastasia?" she asked.

Then she spotted the little tan dog. She was standing at the water's edge, her small black feet planted firmly in the sand, and staring fixedly out at the waves.

11

That evening, Bonnie finished Mr. Conner's book and started pondering once more the events of the day.

It always began, she mused, with that odd sleepiness, then the colors spreading on the waves and finally the glowing aqua pool. And then, and then...*She* was there. It was extraordinary; it was unbelievable; but it seemed Mermaid Island had an actual mermaid! And perhaps Bonnie was the only one who knew of her.

She considered the possibility that she'd imagined the whole incident of the face in the waves. She had been so groggy at the time and since then the details had wavered in her mind, as if they were fading into a memory or a dream.

But what about the pearl? And Carlotta Anastasia? Carlotta Anastasia had definitely seen something. The little dog's body had been quivering with excitement, her curly tail wagging madly. Dogs couldn't see colors, could they? Carlotta Anastasia must have seen something beyond odd colors in the water.

Besides, it was the same face she'd dreamed the other night. But had it been a dream?

Bonnie was inclined now to believe it wasn't. She thought the mermaid had paid her a visit and then came back while she and Moonie were sitting at Yeoman's Beach.

But Moonie wouldn't admit a thing. Bonnie had asked her on the way back to town if she ever saw anything other than the colors in the water, and Moonie had denied it. Bonnie felt strangely reluctant to ask her directly if she'd ever seen a mermaid. Moonie would probably think she was crazy.

But was that all it was? Every time Bonnie opened her mouth to say "mermaid," something stopped her. She felt somehow as if keeping to herself what she had seen was immensely important, but she didn't know why.

Bonnie jumped to her feet. She had to try to see the mermaid again. That was the only way to know for absolutely certain.

Her mother was tapping away at the computer in the corner room, and dusk was stealing over the water when Bonnie went to her jewel case and drew out two more of the glass beads.

Slipping them in her pocket, she crept down to the beach and, as before, tucked them into the hollow in the fallen tree. Then seating herself on the sand, she crossed her legs and prepared to wait.

Fifteen minutes passed, then half an hour. The sun was really sinking now and a chill crept over Bonnie's arms.

She rubbed her hands together to warm them and settled herself more deeply in the sand. Just then a deep maroon begin to grow along the edge of the water near the tree. Forgetting the cold, Bonnie leaped to her feet and took several steps toward the log, staring at the glowing aqua pool now spreading among the branches.

"Oh please," she begged desperately, as she felt sleepiness begin to drag at her eyelids. "Oh please, don't get tired now!"

Struggling to keep her eyes open, she clenched her fingers around the pearl and planted her feet firmly, trying not to sway. Out in the water, the beautiful woman was appearing again in the waves, her silver hair blending with the moonlit crests of the tossing water.

Her eyes, now green, now a glowing sapphire, moved slowly over Bonnie's astonished face.

For a moment they simply looked at each other. Then Bonnie forced her lips to form the words, "Who are you?"

Later, she wished she had said something more clever. After all, it wasn't every day one carried on a conversation with a mermaid.

But the fantastic creature hovering in the waves seemed to notice nothing unusual. Instead, she smiled slightly, and between her pink lips Bonnie saw the most startlingly white teeth.

When she answered, her voice was musical and soft, rushing somehow like the water. Almost not like a voice at all.

"I am of the water," her voice whispered and sang. "I come from the waves off the beach you call Yeoman's."

"But..." Bonnie hesitated. The sleepiness was gone, she noticed suddenly. When had that happened? "I mean, where did you come from? Do other people know you are here?"

The mermaid smiled again.

"I am of the water," she repeated. "I live in the water and come from the water. We are always there, but only a few can actually see us. Most sense us only in their love of the sound of the waves on the beach."

Bonnie stared at her. Was she solid, or could she see just a bit of the evening sky shimmering behind the mermaid's hair?

"Why can I see you?" asked Bonnie at last. Was she asking too many questions? Would she frighten the mermaid away?

But the mermaid did not appear alarmed. Instead, she remained in the bright pool of colors with her shoulders above the water and her glowing gaze fixed curiously on Bonnie, her arms resting quietly on top of the waves.

Curled about the mermaid's body, Bonnie could glimpse the faint outline of her jade-green tail, shining silver in the growing moonlight.

She answered only, "Some can see us; most cannot."

"Are there more of you?"

"More...yes," answered the mermaid, and she sighed, the sound like the murmur of water flowing. "But not many more. Many have gone."

"Gone? Where?" asked Bonnie.

"Gone...away," said the creature, shaking her head so her silver hair spread starlit and glinting over the water. She seemed to think for a moment, then she went on, "We cannot live where the water cannot live."

"You mean if the water goes away?" ventured Bonnie. She didn't understand.

"No," the mermaid seemed to be struggling to explain, "We must live where the water does. When the water dies, then we go away."

Bonnie ventured walking a couple of steps closer and saw the mermaid's form begin to shimmer and the colors go transparent.

"Don't leave," she begged. "I just want to see you better. You are very different from me—from humans."

"You are of the flesh," answered the mermaid's voice, becoming very distant. "We are of the water. You must never tell of us. You must never, ever tell."

"I won't tell," promised Bonnie, "I just..."

But what did she want? She had wished to see the mermaid better, so she could explain about her to her mother, or to Bobbie.

But the mermaid's form no longer seemed substantial. Her shape was wavering in the moonlight and becoming rippled, like water when a pebble is dropped into it.

What was more, Bonnie's sleepiness had returned, and she pinched herself rather desperately.

"Our only defense..." came the mermaid's voice from far, far away, and Bonnie saw her long tail slide silently into the waves, "...is your dreams. When you wake, you may believe you never saw me."

"I will never tell," cried Bonnie. "I will keep your secret."

"Sssssecret," came a whisper from the water. The mermaid was gone. Only a soft mist, colored with rose in the moonlight, remained. "Keep our secret…"

12

When Bonnie sprinted into the house a few minutes later, she found her mother hard at work at the computer, with the printer chugging away next to her.

Bonnie skidded to a halt in the doorway, her heart pumping and her mind whirling. She wanted to blurt out what had just happened on the beach, but the mermaid's warning stopped her.

"You must never, ever tell," the hushed voice echoed in her mind. "Keep our secret."

But keep a secret from her mother? Bonnie had never done that. What should she do? Would the mermaid be in danger if she told just one person?

What had she meant when she said, "Many are gone." Would this mermaid go, too, if Bonnie told the secret? Or might she die?!

"Grab those flyers I printed, Bonnie," called Caro Campbell, interrupting Bonnie's rather frantic train of thought.

Troubled, Bonnie went to pick up a pile of brightly printed papers out of the printer tray.

"PROTEST THE YEOMAN'S BEACH DEVELOPMENT. PROTECT MERMAID ISLAND'S PRECIOUS NATURAL AREAS," she read. The posters noted the time and place of the Village Council meeting and urged concerned citizens to come and make their voices heard.

"We need to get the word out about what's happening," said Bonnie's mother, waving one of the flyers, "so people can speak out against the development!"

"What have you found out?" asked Bonnie.

"It's a private company that wants to build on Yeoman's Beach," her mother answered, "hired by an anonymous investor. The plan is to put in cabins and private weekend homes with boat decks, plus the heliport."

"But a heliport is silly!" protested Bonnie.

"I know," said her mother wryly, shaking her head. "It's very strange. It isn't meant for a commercial development, either. Whoever is doing this has a *lot* of money."

"But what's it for?" asked Bonnie.

"We don't know," answered her mother. "The developer has turned over what they're required to, but we don't know what's behind it really."

Bonnie frowned. What had the mermaid said? "We are of the water. And when the water no longer lives, then we must go." Her stomach churned. What would happen to the mermaid if houses were built along the beach?

"Are the cabins to go near the water?" she demanded.

"Right on the beach," answered her mother grimly. "Spread out so they're nice and private for the residents, but of course it's devastating for the natural habitat. And all those flowers. I saw three endangered ones out that way a few days ago. I probably should add some notes to my inventory..."

Bonnie stopped listening. Her mother was off in her own world, talking to herself in an undertone and bustling around the room.

Bonnie carried the flyers out to the kitchen table and flopped down in a chair. Sighing, she put her chin in her hand. So much had happened, and she had the feeling there was something important she was missing. She just needed to concentrate and work it out. But somehow her brain felt foggy, and the encounter with the mermaid had already faded, as if she had been dreaming.

A dream! She shook herself. That's what the mermaid had said would happen! "Our only defense is your dreams." Would she eventually decide she had imagined the whole thing? But it was not a dream. It was not!

Her mother strode into the room and dropped some posters down on the table.

"I'm going to hang some of these around town tomorrow," she announced, and pointed to the ones in front of Bonnie. "Why don't you tack some up, too. The Frollop Shop, the library. Give some to Bobbie VanGelderen and her family to spread around."

"Okay," agreed Bonnie. Perhaps telling her mother about the mermaid could wait. She set a handful of posters on top of her backpack. "The meeting's less than three weeks away. We don't have much time."

"Right," said her mother. "But a lot can happen in three weeks! We'll fight this, Bonnie. And we'll win!"

Her mother went back into the corner room, and soon Bonnie could hear her on the computer, her fingers flying over the keys. She was murmuring to herself and shuffling papers, back to her research project.

Bonnie sighed again, feeling worried and sad. Now there was a new reason not to develop Yeoman's. If houses were built on the beach, what would happen to the strange and wonderful being who lived in the waves?

Her mind racing with thoughts of the mermaid and worry about the Yeoman's Beach problems, she reached idly across the table and picked up the Island News. It had an article about a new spaghetti restaurant on Main Street, and an editorial discussing the Yeoman's development.

Bonnie scanned the editorial. It gave very few details. In fact, it wasn't nearly as negative as Bonnie thought it might be. The writer pointed out that after all, it wasn't a high-density development that was proposed. Perhaps the effect on the environment would be minimal.

Bonnie turned the page in disgust.

To her delight, the next section, "Entertainment," had a long article about Gregor McNaughton's new movie, where it was being filmed, and how the production was progressing. There were several photos of the handsome actor smiling his famous smile.

"I wonder how Gregor McNaughton feels about the Yeoman's rezoning," wondered Bonnie suddenly. "After all, Yeoman's is practically in his back yard. He'd be a good person to have on our side."

Her mind racing, Bonnie jumped to her feet and ran up to her bedroom. She reached for the telephone, then glanced at the time and decided it was too late to call Bobbie.

Could they approach Gregor McNaughton for help? Could they write him a letter, or put a message on his gate post? It seemed as if he might be a powerful ally, but how to do it? Bobbie might have an idea.

"I just know this will work!" Bonnie thought excitedly. "Gregor McNaughton can save Yeoman's Beach!"

With that happy thought in mind, she put on her pajamas and crawled under her covers, pulling the sheet up to her chin against the chill of the island nighttime air. Outside she could hear the water surging and flowing in its never-ending race toward the shore. Beneath that restless surface the most amazing creature Bonnie had ever imagined danced and swirled with the surging waves. It was up to Bonnie to save her.

13

Bonnie awoke with the dawn the next morning, yanking on her shorts and a t-shirt and dashing down to the kitchen before her mother had finished yawning over her first cup of coffee.

"Where are you going today?" asked Bonnie, while she ponytailed her hair in the hallway mirror.

"Back to the north side of the island," answered Caro Campbell, staring curiously at her daughter. "What's got you up so bright and early?"

"I got the most wonderful idea last night, mom!" exclaimed Bonnie, sitting down across from her mother at the table. "It could save Yeoman's!"

"What is it?" inquired her mother.

"We'll get the help of Gregor McNaughton," Bonnie answered excitedly. "With his 'secret' home over near the beach, he won't want a bunch of new houses going in. He's got so much money and power I know he could help. But how can we let him know how much of an emergency it is?" Bonnie rubbed her brow. "He isn't even here. He's in Italy working on his new movie. I was thinking Bobbie and I could write him or something."

"That's an good plan, Bonnie," answered her mother, "if you can reach him. But now that I think of it," her forehead wrinkled suddenly, "Wouldn't you suppose his staff would keep him informed of island happenings? Seems as if he'd have stepped forward by now."

"Maybe he's busy filming," speculated Bonnie. She gave the newspaper a push. "This article even tells what town they're in. It would be great if he took a break and flew back for the meeting," she added eagerly.

"I wonder," said Bonnie's mother slowly. "But it can't hurt, anyway. Just don't pester him, if he's so determined to have his privacy."

"We won't," promised Bonnie.

Her mother went to the sink to rinse her cup. "I've got to get a move on if I'm going to get any work done before it gets hot," she commented.

She looked up from shoving a sandwich into a paper bag and smiled at Bonnie. "What do you say to the two of us taking a little side trip after I finish my project? Maybe do some shopping on the mainland? Catch a couple of movies?"

Bonnie smiled back. "That would be great, mom, but if you're saying that because you think I'm having a boring summer, I'm not. I'm really not!"

Caro Campbell returned Bonnie's smile and ruffled her daughter's hair. "That's partly why I said it, but partly I'd just like to spend some time with you. I'm so glad you're having a good summer."

Her mother put on her heavy boots, shouldered her backpack and the computer, and headed out the door, blowing Bonnie a kiss.

Bonnie gave Bobbie another half an hour to sleep in and then telephoned her house. She found Bobbie already up and chattering about her shopping trip.

"I got a ton of school clothes," she gushed, "and some new music CD's and a computer game. Want to come over and see them?"

"I'd really like that," answered Bonnie, "And I've got something to tell you, too. I had the most wonderful idea. I need to go to town first, though, and hang posters. My mom made up a bunch of them for saving Yeoman's."

"Why don't you come for lunch?" offered Bobbie, "and bring some posters with you. My dad can put them up at work and I'll put some around, too."

"Okay," agreed Bonnie.

She gathered up the posters, a pad of paper, pens, and a large roll of tape. Throwing everything into her backpack, she headed out the door and toward town. The day promised to be sunny and hot, and Bonnie lifted her face toward the slight breeze.

What did mermaids do when it got hot? Did they notice climate changes? What about the winter? Did the water around Mermaid Island freeze in the winter? If it did, where would the mermaid go then? She had so many questions, but most of all she wanted to know if anyone else had ever seen a mermaid on the island.

"Some can see us; most cannot," the mermaid had said. But a lot of people could see the colors. And the colors in the waves and the mermaid were definitely connected.

"Our only defense is your dreams." Somehow the mermaids had the ability to dull the senses, and anyone who did actually see them thought they'd dreamed the experience.

What about Mr. Conner? His book hadn't mentioned the mermaids at all, although there was a section talking about the beautiful colors many had reported seeing in the waves...crests tipped with green and rose and copper; deep drifts of purple and magenta. He had explained it as a trick of the island sunshine, just as Moonie had. But Moonie knew more than she was telling, Bonnie was sure of it.

Bonnie hung posters in the windows of the Frollop Shop, the new spaghetti shop, and the laundry, then headed for the library. Inside, she put two posters on public bulletin boards, and left half a dozen on the "resources" table.

On an impulse, she headed for the local history section again. Scanning the titles, most of which were simply books about island life that mentioned Mermaid Island, she found tucked in an end section of the bookshelf a slim blue volume with gold writing on the cover. It was entitled Mermaid Musings: Random Recollections of Life on the Island. Gently flipping open the cover, Bonnie read that it was published in 1917, by Mary Montrose.

It was a diary! If there was information about mermaid sightings anywhere, that would be where she'd find it, Bonnie thought excitedly. She hurried up to the counter and asked if she could check it out.

"Oh, that's a rare book, so we don't let it leave the library," answered Mr. Conner, "But you're welcome to read it here. Mrs. Montrose lived on Mermaid Island for many years," he went on. "She and her husband are both buried here, out in the island cemetery."

Bonnie glanced at her watch. 10:30AM. She had time to look through the book for a while before meeting Bobbie for lunch. Carrying it to a quiet corner, she set her backpack on the floor next to her and curled up in a comfortable chair. Flipping open the cover, she began to read.

14

An hour later, Bonnie had returned the book to the shelf and was running toward Bobbie's house as fast as she could, balancing her jouncing backpack.

Her thoughts were racing. Mrs. Montrose had pages and pages and pages of interesting diary entries. Her husband had fought overseas in World War I, and his lonely wife spent hours on the beach writing her memoirs.

The entries had stopped abruptly when Mr. Montrose had returned, wounded but alive, but the writing she'd done in those earlier years was a fascinating and detailed story of Mermaid Island life–both natural history and village history. She had not written of seeing a mermaid, but had written a great deal about the colors.

The whole island had been surrounded by waves touched with all the colors of the rainbow, Mrs. Montrose had noted, but as the village grew, especially when the row of shoreline restaurants was built, the colors receded. The waves still had colors, but they were subtle and faded.

And then the most chilling entry of all, where Mrs. Montrose had noted sadly, "In places it's as if the water has died, and the colors are only a memory."

If what Mrs. Montrose wrote was true, thought Bonnie, as she hurried along the road, then when houses were built on the Yeoman's shoreline, the mermaids would die.

The thought frightened Bonnie so that she began to jog again, and soon she arrived breathlessly in front of Bobbie's blue door. Panting, she rang the bell.

Bobbie let her in, bubbling with stories about her mall visit and modeling a very pretty blue shirt with gold trim on the sleeves. Though Bonnie tried to listen politely to her friend's excited chatter, she was having a hard time concentrating.

It was funny, Bonnie mused, how she hadn't really cared much that Bobbie had gone to the mall without her. A few short weeks ago, spending the summer away from the city had seemed like a prison sentence. Now she was as wrapped up in Mermaid Island as if she had lived here her whole life.

Bonnie could smell the delicious aroma of chocolate chip cookies baking in the kitchen, and Moonie came striding in a few minutes later munching on a ball of cookie dough, Carlotta Anastasia at her heels.

Glancing at Bonnie's rather forlorn face, Moonie commented, "What's the matter, Bonnie? You look sad."

Bobbie halted in mid-sentence and stared at Bonnie in concern.

"Yes, what's the matter, Bonnie?" she echoed.

Carlotta Anastasia put her front feet up on Bonnie's knee, and Bonnie knelt to stroke her fat little body.

"It's the Yeoman's Beach development," she sighed. "We just have to do something to save the beach. They can't build houses there, they can't!"

"What's happened?" asked Bobbie and Moonie simultaneously, then looked at each other and giggled.

"Come have a cookie. Aunt Polly and I have been baking all morning," said Moonie, and the three friends went into the kitchen.

Moonie set out tray of warm cookies and then sat down. The other two joined her at the table.

Reaching for a cookie, Bonnie told them what she had read in Mrs. Montrose's journal. "And the thing is," she added, glancing at Moonie, "She said it was as if the water had died."

Bobbie glanced from Bonnie to Moonie and frowned. "I wish I could see the colors," she said sadly. "It makes me so mad that I can't. That is, I can see colors, but I know you guys see something different."

"Some can; most cannot," said Moonie and Bonnie glanced at her sharply.

Moonie's sparkling hazel eyes were looking steadily into Bonnie's brown ones, and then Bonnie realized what Moonie was doing.

"Keep our secret. You must never, ever tell," the mermaid had said, and Moonie wouldn't. She wouldn't tell even if she thought someone else had seen the same thing she had. A secret was a secret, and that was that.

If the word got out that there were mermaids in the waves on Mermaid Island, people would come, and where there were people, there were houses and developments, and where there were houses and developments, the water could not live. Yeoman's natural area had to be protected. It was the last place the mermaids had.

Bonnie jumped to her feet, clutching her cookie. "I had a great idea last night!" she said, and then rushed on, "What if we got word to Gregor McNaughton about the development and made him understand how important it is for him to help us? My mom says he probably already knows what's going on, but maybe he thinks the Village Council will turn the proposal down and he doesn't need to worry. But what if they don't? I mean, I read an article in the paper last night and whoever wrote it didn't seem to think the development was such a bad idea. I wonder if it might pass? Do you think it's possible it might?" Bonnie moaned.

Moonie and Bobbie exchanged glances. "Bonnie's right. We need to do something," said Moonie. "And Gregor McNaughton might be just the person to help. He'd have money for a really big publicity campaign and he must have a lot of friends that could join in the fight."

"My mom says he has a foundation that supports important causes," offered Bobbie.

"Great!" said Bonnie and Moonie together.

"But we have to hurry!" wailed Bonnie. "The meeting is coming up pretty quickly."

"We need to get word to Mr. McNaughton somehow," said Bobbie. "Maybe we should write him a letter."

"I'll bet his letters go off to some secretary or something, like fan mail," said Moonie. "He may never even read them."

"But doesn't even someone famous have to pay an electric bill or anything?" demanded Bonnie. "He must have an address."

"I know how to find out!" announced Bobbie. "Let's go check his gate. There might be a number on it. Or maybe he's got a private letter box. We could put a note in there."

"Good idea!" said Moonie. She bounded to her feet. "I've got my camera with me. I'll take a photo of his house for you, Bonnie, if you like. You can take it back with you when you leave at the end of the summer and show your friends in school."

"I'd like that," said Bonnie, although the idea of leaving the island suddenly didn't seem all that happy a thought.

She'd grown to love it here, and with the mermaid it was the most special place in the world.

Bobbie and Moonie tied on sneakers, and Moonie set Carlotta Anastasia firmly in the living room by Polly's feet.

"You stay with Aunt Polly," she told her pet. "We don't need a little dog slowing us down."

Carlotta Anastasia looked rather offended at that, but she settled down quickly enough, especially after Bobbie's mother handed her a bite of cookie.

"Let's go," said Bobbie, and she headed out the front door, Bonnie and Moonie trailing after her. Moonie slung her camera over her shoulder.

For a while, the three girls tramped silently along the gravel road, deep in thought. Then Bobbie spoke.

"Let's put a poster on the gate while we're there," she suggested. "We'll want to send him more information, but right now there's no time to be lost."

"Right," said Bonnie, and they walked determinedly on. Moonie fiddled with her camera, loading new film for Bonnie's photo of Gregor McNaughton's house.

At last they rounded a bend in the road and Bobbie pointed ahead.

15

"It's just up there," she said. "The entrance is by those bushes."

Bonnie stopped short and stood with her jaw dropped, staring at the light glinting off the gate.

"Er–that isn't solid gold is it?" she asked, staring at the scrolled bars across the top of the structure.

"I'm sure it's not," Bobbie assured her. "Maybe just gold plate or something?" She giggled at the expression on Bonnie's face.

"I've never seen anything like it!" said Bonnie.

"I told you it was huge!" exclaimed Bobbie. "It's the most amazing place I've ever seen."

The house, painted a glistening white, shimmered gently in the distance, partly hidden by the light woods behind the gate. A long porch with tall pillars gave way to a deep, sloping lawn, dotted here and there with ornamental bushes and flowering plants. The paved drive curved toward them. It was lined with tall trees, their leaves fluttering gently in the slight breeze. The metal gate, flanked by tall brick posts, was topped with a security camera aimed toward the drive. A brick wall stretched away on either side of the gate, curling back into the forest and enclosing Mr. McNaughton's property.

"I'd say he likes his privacy!" exclaimed Bonnie. "This looks like a fort!"

"Doesn't it?" answered Bobbie.

Moonie had chosen a spot in the road with a good view and had snapped a couple of photos of the gate and up the driveway. Just as she was walking farther away to get a better shot of the house, Bobbie hissed, "There's a car coming up the drive!" and dove for the bushes.

"What are you doing?!" gasped Bonnie, who had scrambled in after her.

Moonie crashed into the two of them seconds later, and the friends huddled together deep in the sheltering leaves.

"What are you doing?" repeated Bonnie. "Why are we hiding?"

"I'm not quite sure," Bobbie answered, rather embarrassed. "Somehow I thought it would be better if no one saw us. That's silly, isn't it?"

"We were on a public road," answered Moonie stoutly, and began to stand up. "We aren't doing anything wrong."

But Bobbie grabbed her arm and pulled her cousin back into a crouch. The gate had begun to creak open.

"Let's just wait," Bobbie said. "Now I feel dumb. If we come out, maybe they'll think we were up to something."

"Bobbie, you dope!" exclaimed Moonie, but she stayed kneeling. "I hope they leave quickly."

Bonnie said nothing. She wished they had never come. What if someone saw them hiding? Nervously, she fingered her grandmother's pearl.

The car paused at the gate, and Bonnie squinted through the leaves at the man inside. He was handsome and well-dressed, wearing a light green polo shirt and belted khaki shorts. His longish black hair was slightly ruffled by the wind.

To her surprise, he stepped out of the car, leaving it running, and gazed in the direction of town, shading his eyes with his hand.

"There's another car coming," whispered Bobbie, who had a better view of the road.

"This is awful," gasped Moonie. "I am so embarrassed."

"Just keep quiet," Bobbie poked Moonie. "They'll be gone in a minute."

But instead of driving by, the second car rolled to a stop in front of the gate. It was a light blue sedan, driven by a man in a straw cowboy hat.

"That's Mr. Veenstra!" whispered Bobbie. "What would he being doing here?"

"Shhhh," breathed Moonie.

"What kept you?" snapped the well-dressed man from Mr. McNaughton's house.

If she hadn't been so frightened, Bonnie might have considered that an unfair question, since he had just driven up the driveway himself.

"Sorry," answered Mr. Veenstra, but he didn't actually sound very sorry. In fact, he sounded annoyed and unhappy. "I had a meeting, and then people were around and I couldn't break away."

He glanced up the road, and the three girls melted farther back into the bushes.

"There's a strong campaign to block the development," Mr. Veenstra went on, "And I don't mind saying it could be successful. I'm only one vote, you know!"

"You're responsible for that, Veenstra. Fix it!" snarled the other man. He pulled out his wallet and began counting out a thick wad of bills.

Beside her, Bonnie heard the quiet whir of Moonie's little instant camera, then another whir and another. Moonie was balanced up on her heels, the lens pointed at the two men, and she was snapping photo after photo.

Bonnie was breathing so hard she was afraid they could hear her back in the village. She held her fingers over her mouth and tried not to gulp. She had never been so terrified in her life. Was Mr. Veenstra accepting a bribe?

"We're paying you to make this come out right," the man from the house continued in a vicious undertone. "Don't mess it up! The developer already has his money, and Mr. McNaughton sent a FAX today authorizing the final payment. He wants those houses in there quickly, so he can have his friends come to the island to stay without being pestered by the press."

The man slapped the bills into Mr. Veenstra's hand and Bonnie heard Moonie's camera whir again.

"Take care of it, Veenstra," he snapped. "If this deal doesn't work, you'll be sorry."

Mr. Veenstra looked angry, but he also looked afraid, Bonnie saw. His face had flushed a deep red.

"I'll do what I can, Paxton," said Mr. Veenstra. "But I'm not going to prison for this. I've got a family to support. If you don't lay off me, I'll tell the paper you paid me to try to fix the vote."

"That would be unwise," said Paxton, in a voice that made Bonnie shiver. How could Moonie stay so calm? She'd been shooting photos, intently and deliberately, during the entire exchange between the two men.

Mr. Veenstra uttered something that could have been a threat, though it was so said quietly that Bonnie couldn't hear what it was. Then he strode back to his car and with a spray of gravel spun around in a circle, heading back toward town.

Paxton pulled a cellular phone out of his pocket and pressed some buttons.

Bonnie heard him say, "Get me Gregor in Italy." Then he, too, got into his car and, reversing quickly, sped back up the drive.

16

As soon as the cars were out of sight, the terrified trio burst out of the bushes and ran for Yeoman's Beach, their feet pounding along the narrow wooded path.

When they finally reached the long stretch of white sand, they collapsed in the comforting warmth, panting and perspiring. Moonie was clutching her little camera and a handful of paper strips that held the photos she had taken of Mr. Veenstra and Paxton.

The first one to speak was Bobbie.

"That snake!" she said through her teeth. "That lowdown, slimy snake! He's taking money from Paxton to influence the Village Council! I don't think I've ever been so scared or so angry!"

Bonnie nodded, putting a hand on her lurching stomach.

Hiding there in the bushes had been one of the hardest things she'd ever done. "Gregor McNaughton's in on it," she said at last. "He's been sending Paxton instructions from Italy!"

Meanwhile, Moonie had begun gently peeling the paper backings off the photos, guarding the precious images from the bright sunlight and sand.

"I caught everything," she said grimly, and Bonnie and Bobbie scrambled over to see. "I got Paxton handing Mr. Veenstra the money, I got them talking, I got Mr. Veenstra's face all red."

At that, Bobbie gave a nervous giggle. "He was really angry, wasn't he?"

Bonnie giggled along with her, although she was still very frightened. What if one if the men had seen them hiding in the bushes? She didn't like to think of what might have happened.

Moonie slid the photos carefully into her camera case so as not to scratch the images, and then sat back on her heels. The three girls looked anxiously at each other.

Bonnie said quickly, "We need to tell our parents right away. They'll know how to handle this!"

Moonie nodded. "Let's go."

The friends got to their feet and began to hurry along the beach in the direction of town, keeping to the shade along the shoreline. From the corner of her eye, Bonnie kept watch in the direction of the road where it ran behind the trees. They were a long way from Gregor McNaughton's home now, but the thought of Paxton suddenly jumping out of the bushes was terrifying.

When they finally left the beach path and entered the village, they stayed to the side streets and out of sight until they had to cut past the Frollop Shop and the Town Hall. Then they ran quickly toward Main Street and were nearly to safety when suddenly Mr. Veenstra emerged from the spaghetti shop and nearly bowled into Bonnie.

Bonnie gasped and felt the blood drain from her face. She opened her mouth, but absolutely no sound would emerge.

Suddenly she felt Moonie grab her arm and say, "Hello Mr. Veenstra!" in her brightest voice.

Mr. Veenstra barely glanced at them. His face was like a storm cloud under his straw hat, and Bonnie could see one of his hands was clenched into a fist.

But he answered, "Afternoon, Moonie VanGelderen," in such a normal voice that Bonnie let out the breath she'd been holding.

They were safe for now!

They hurried on down the road as quickly as they could without looking suspicious, but Bonnie couldn't resist one look over her shoulder as they rounded the corner by the Frollop Shop. She saw Mr. Veenstra clamber into his car and speed up the road in the opposite direction.

"Whew!" Bobbie said. Her red hair was all askew and her cheeks were pink with exertion. "I've had one too many close calls today! You don't think he noticed anything, do you?"

"I don't think so," answered Bonnie. "I think he's concentrating on his own troubles."

"I'm going home to find my mom," said Moonie.

"My mom's working out in the woods," said Bonnie rather plaintively, and her eyes stung for a moment.

Right now she wanted nothing more than to throw herself into her mother's arms. She had relived over and over the awful moments while they were crouching in the bushes, and her heart was still pounding.

Bobbie squeezed her hand in understanding. In fact, she looked rather close to tears herself all of a sudden, and as Moonie jogged over to her house next door Bobbie put her arm over Bonnie's shoulders.

"Come on inside," she said to her friend, and Bonnie nodded gratefully. "Aunt Bettina will know how to reach your mom."

Polly expressed shock and horror at the girls' experience. While she listened to them repeat their story, she gave them each a cold glass of lemonade and several cookies, then she phoned next door to talk to Moonie's mother.

"Can you believe it?" Polly exclaimed into the receiver. "He's not going to get away with it! Not while there's a VanGelderen left on this island! What shall we do first, Bettina?"

There was a pause while she listened, then, "Yes, I agree. Bonnie's here right now. The girls are so upset. Let me know what she says...Yes...I know she will...Talk later...Bye."

Bobbie's mom put her hands on her hips and furrowed her brow.

"That Nick Veenstra's going to be very sorry he tried to cross this town. His wife's the sweetest thing ever. I can't believe what a rat he turned out to be. Bonnie, honey, Bettina's going to see if she can find your mom out on the north side and bring her over for a war party. You're welcome to stay here until then."

"Thanks, I'd like that," said Bonnie in a small voice. She shivered, and Polly handed her another cookie.

"Nothing like chocolate chips to make you feel better," she said. "You girls did a brave thing today, and you may very well have saved our whole island. Who knows where Gregor McNaughton would stop? His next trick might be even worse!"

"I know," said Bonnie, but privately she thought this one was bad enough. What was the mermaid thinking and doing right now?

Polly was bustling around the kitchen and muttering, "He can't use his money and his power to push us around. We islanders won't take that! If he wants a place for his buddies to have private parties, then he can just use his money to build it somewhere else!"

She looked so fierce that Bonnie suddenly began to feel better and she smiled tentatively at Bobbie. Bobbie grinned back and took a big bite of her cookie.

By that evening, the story had been told and re-told and the two VanGelderen families and Caro and Bonnie Campbell had talked themselves hoarse plotting and planning and re-planning. Nothing remained of two large pizzas but a few crumbs, and Bonnie suddenly found herself feeling drowsy. Seeing her daughter's drooping eyelids, Bonnie's mother excused them to start for home.

"Are you okay, honey?" she asked.

She hadn't bothered to remove her field boots in her haste to get to the VanGelderens' house, and the heavy soles clumped along the drive as they made their way to the car.

"I'm okay," replied Bonnie. "Just tired. It was really scary hiding there in the bushes. I didn't know what was going to happen. Isn't it a miracle Moonie thought to take those photos?"

Caro Campbell reached for her daughter's hand. "It sure is," she said. "But you were all wonderful. Your quick thinking is going to save Yeoman's Beach."

"I hope so, mom," said Bonnie. "I sure hope so."

For a few minutes they drove along in silence. Bonnie stared out at the fading sunshine, thinking about the mermaid.

Then her mother said sadly, "Bonnie, I am so sorry all this has happened. I had hoped this would turn out to be a wonderful summer, and now I almost wish we had never come!"

Bonnie thought for a moment, and then answered firmly, "Well, I really wish today hadn't happened, but other than that I wouldn't trade this summer for anything. I love it here, Mom! Especially the beach and the water. I wish the summer could last longer, in fact!"

Her mother glanced fondly at Bonnie and smiled. "Then it's a dream come true for me, after all," she said at last. "Let's do something fun to take our minds off this bad day."

"Okay," agreed Bonnie, "What shall we do?"

"Hey!" said her mother suddenly. "What about the Frollop Shop? Maybe tonight is my chance to try one. And after all," she continued, "we need to build up our strength for the fight to save Yeoman's."

Bonnie laughed for the first time in what seemed like hours.

"Then we'd better stop," she answered. "Now let me explain the flavors. Bobbie likes a variety, while my special favorite is watermelon, and Moonie really likes pear…"

17

Later that night, Bonnie began to think about Yeoman's Beach and she tossed and turned and twisted in bed, wakeful and restless. Finally she drifted into a light sleep, only to be jerked awake at sunrise by a most fearsome nightmare.

Looking out the window of her room, she saw the first rays of the morning sun stealing across the water and she clambered out of bed, tiptoeing to her closet and pulling a jacket on over her pajamas.

It was Saturday, and her mother wasn't working in the field. Instead, her Saturday routine was to get up later than usual, drink a cup of coffee over the morning paper, then head to the computer room to write, organize her database and Web surf looking for references.

Bonnie let herself out the front door and into the chilly dawn, drawn to the water and the beach. Making her way along the narrow path, she found herself on the north end of Yeoman's, the long stretch of sand stretching silent and empty before her and the water lapping gently at the shore in an early-morning moment of stillness, as if resting before the wind picked up.

Bonnie sat down on a log and looked out at the water.

"Are you there?" she asked quietly, and almost immediately the waves began to swirl and flow with color, lapping and rolling around a bright aqua center.

The extraordinary face of the mermaid arose out of the waves, her hair spread fanlike on the water and her arms glistening in the early morning light. Today there were tiny pinpoints of green glowing at her throat and around her wrists, as if she'd put on some sort of enchanted jewelry.

Bonnie gazed at her, fighting the odd sleepiness until it finally gave way and she could concentrate without effort.

"Something awful has happened," she blurted out. "Something that could affect you and your people."

The lovely face stayed calm. The mermaid's eyes, now blue, now deep green, rested gently on

Bonnie's hands, which were twisting against her stomach.

"What has happened?" she finally asked, and as before her voice seemed to come out of nowhere and everywhere, echoing and reflecting the music of the waves.

"Someone is trying to build homes on the beach," said Bonnie. "Someone very powerful."

The mermaid cocked her head, but said nothing. She had raised her gaze to Bonnie's face now, and her look was sad, but peaceful.

"That has happened before," she sighed.

"The water will change, and you will go away," cried Bonnie, and tears began to run down her cheeks.

The mermaid held out her arms, and Bonnie saw with amazement that her tears appeared to be dropping slowly into the mermaid's hands, where they glittered in her curled fingers like diamonds. The mermaid gazed at the tears for a moment, then held out her hands and scattered the tears around her on the water. There they glimmered and sparkled gold and silver like a jeweled necklace.

Bonnie stared, open-mouthed.

"How did you do that?" Bonnie gasped, but the mermaid just smiled at her, such a smile as Bonnie had never seen—bright and joyous.

"You weep for us!" she said, in her strange, hollow voice. "I have never seen this, though others have told me of it."

Bonnie nodded and another tear slid down, going to join its fellows in the tossing surf, glinting in the water.

"I am afraid what will happen to you," Bonnie wept. "You are so special, and so fragile. What if the water dies?"

"If the water dies, we will go away," said the mermaid calmly. "But you have given us a precious gift. The gift of your tears."

"I will try to help you," promised Bonnie. "I'll do everything I can."

Again that beautiful smile. "Then all will be well," the mermaid murmured against the rising wind. "I shall keep your tears with me always."

And then she was gone. A faint mist hovered above the water where her shoulders had risen from the waves, glimmering rose and indigo in the growing sunlight.

Bonnie walked slowly back to the cabin, suddenly wanting desperately to go back to sleep. She was bone-tired from her restless night, fright and worry. But seeing the mermaid had reassured her. She thought she could sleep now.

As she approached the house, Bonnie saw her mother standing at the window, watching as she walked up the path.

"Are you all right?" she asked when Bonnie entered the house.

"I'm all right," Bonnie answered. "I just wanted to walk on the beach for a minute."

"I heard you leave," said her mother gently. "I made you some hot chocolate. But you look ready to go back to bed."

"I will," promised Bonnie, "but hot chocolate sounds good first."

She slid a kitchen chair out from the table with her foot and sat down, resting her chin on her crossed arms.

"Mom," she said. "I have a secret."

"Do you?" answered her mother mildly, pouring the chocolate into a cup. "Secrets are fun."

"I don't know if I should tell you," said Bonnie uncomfortably. "I've never kept a secret like this."

Bonnie's mom put the steaming mug down on the table and then sat across from her daughter.

"Well, let's think," she said. "Could anyone be hurt if you don't tell?"

"I don't think so," answered Bonnie truthfully. "In fact, it really isn't my secret exactly. It's sort of someone else's."

"Would they mind if you told?" asked her mother.

"They told me not to," replied Bonnie, looking sadly into her mother's face. "And bad things might happen if a lot of people find out."

"Then you'd best not tell," Caro Campbell said, smiling. "You've been entrusted with something very, very important—someone's confidence. Keep your secret, and guard it well."

Bonnie smiled back at her. "I will," she said.

"Now," Bonnie's mother pulled her own cup off the counter and set it down on the table. "Before you drop off to sleep, let's talk about the Village Council meeting and how we're going to outfox Nick Veenstra and Gregor McNaughton. We've got lots of work to do, and we need to get busy right away."

Bonnie bent her brown head toward her mother's bright blonde one.

"Now this is what we're going to do..." Caro Campbell said.

18

The days sped by as the three families worked to prepare for the meeting. Bonnie's mother made two trips to the mainland to visit the print shop, the photo shop, and the bank. The phone lines were busy between the Campbells' cabin and the VanGelderen homes, and Bonnie, Bobbie, and Moonie met at the beach every day to talk and compare notes. They spied Mr. Veenstra in town several times looking busy and important. Bonnie always pretended she didn't see him, and he didn't appear to notice.

The Frollop Shop introduced a new flavor, blueberry, and the three friends sampled it. Bobbie pronounced it the best yet, but Moonie stayed true to pear.

Bonnie went often to Yeoman's Beach and sat in the warm sand with her arms folded on her knees.

Sometimes the mermaid came and sometimes she did not, but Bonnie imagined her always dancing and sliding through the water, sparkling and flowing with the waves.

And then the day was upon them. The meeting of the Village Council.

The Town Hall was filled to bursting, every chair taken and residents of Mermaid Island lining the walls. Several people even sat cross-legged on the floor. In front of the room, the council members sat at a large table shuffling papers, murmuring to each other, and gazing out at the restless audience.

Squeezed between her mother and Bobbie in the middle of a row, Bonnie had a clear view of the meeting table between the shoulders of the people in front of her. She had to suppress a scowl at Mr. Veenstra looking so grave and pompous.

Bonnie saw Bettina VanGelderen nudge Caro Campbell with her elbow.

"There's Barb Veenstra," she whispered.

Bonnie looked at Mr. Veenstra's wife, who was sitting off to the side in the front of the room. She held a small blue purse in her lap and wore a smart suit with a flowered blouse. She looked well dressed, kind and very proud of her husband. Bonnie felt sorry for her.

After a few more minutes of waiting, Mr. Veenstra called the meeting to order, and Bonnie felt her mother sit up very straight next to her.

The minutes of the previous meeting were approved, the Treasurer's Report was read, and then it was time to move on to the action agenda.

There was just one item, Mr. Veenstra explained. He introduced the proposal from the developer and pointed to a map to explain the area under discussion.

"As if we had to be told where Yeoman's Beach was!" Moonie hissed to Bobbie.

"The area is, of course, a valuable natural area, but it is also of great commercial interest to the tourism industry," continued Mr. Veenstra. "And luxury, high-rent tourist cabins are what is proposed, stretching along the shoreline from here..." Mr. Veenstra held one finger on the south bend of the beach, "...to here." His finger moved along the line of the water halfway up the area that was Yeoman's.

The room had gone deathly silent when he started speaking, but now it was buzzing angrily, people talking among themselves and pointing up to the front.

Mr. Veenstra asked for quiet, and then asked again, but several people were standing up now, and one gentleman called out.

"Veenstra! Let's hear how you feel about it!"

Mr. Veenstra shifted his weight from foot to foot. "Well," he looked a bit uncomfortable. "The tourist industry has been good for Mermaid Island. Everyone knows that. We just opened a new spaghetti shop and last year we had more day-visitors come over by ferry than ever before."

The room was quiet again, and Mr. Veenstra began to look more confident.

"However, you know my strong feelings about environmental issues and Mermaid Island. Nothing is more important to me!"

Bobbie quivered next to Bonnie. "Do you believe him?" she whispered. "He is just lying and lying!"

Bonnie's mother raised her hand, and Bonnie held her breath, her heart pounding. Two seats down Moonie was craning to see around the woman sitting in front of her. Bobbie's mother and father were holding hands and Polly was smiling slightly.

"Yes?" Mr. Veenstra called on Bonnie's mother, looking rather impatient at the interruption.

Her mother stood up. "May I have a point of personal privilege?" she asked.

Mr. Veenstra's eyes widened. "Discussion about the proposal comes after the presentation. Did you have a question?"

Bobbie poked Bonnie. "What's a point of personal privilege?" she asked.

"It's when you make a personal comment that is not related to the agenda," she whispered. "It's like a little interruption to make a personal observation."

Bobbie turned her eyes back to the front of the room. Mr. Veenstra's face looked rather red.

"I don't have a question. I'd just like a point of personal privilege," Bonnie's mother repeated. "It'll only take a minute."

Mr. Veenstra stared at her, then finally nodded. "Go ahead," he said. He looked as if he wanted to refuse to allow her to speak, but was afraid it would anger the people from the village even more.

Bonnie's mother walked to the front of the room and went to stand near him.

"Nick," she began. "I wanted to take a minute to explain something to the audience."

Mr. Veenstra raised his brows, then nodded jerkily.

"I've been aware for a long time of your interest in environmental concerns, and of your commitment to preserving natural areas on Mermaid Island."

Mr. Veenstra shifted his feet, looking confused but rather pleased.

Bobbie nudged Bonnie with her elbow again and whispered, "He's eating this up!"

"And I know," Bonnie's mother continued, "How difficult—how terribly difficult—this development proposal must be for you, given your knowledge of how it will destroy Yeoman's natural habitat."

Mr. Veenstra opened his mouth, but then closed it again, for Bonnie's mother was smiling and holding out a rolled paper wrapped with a gold band. His brows lowered in confusion, and Bonnie felt Bobbie's hand creep over and hold onto hers. People in the room were beginning to whisper among themselves.

Bonnie's mother raised her hand and the murmuring died away.

"Ladies and gentleman," she said, "I have a special presentation to make tonight."

Now the hall was deathly quiet, all eyes directed at Mr. Veenstra.

"Mr. Veenstra, along with Gregor McNaughton, has been instrumental in preserving Mermaid Island's endangered species and the important natural areas that shelter them."

Mr. Veenstra looked uncomfortable at having his name connected with Gregor McNaughton's and opened his mouth as if to speak, but Bonnie's mother pressed on.

"Thus, on behalf of the residents of Mermaid Island, I present you with this certificate of appreciation. I have a duplicate for Mr. McNaughton."

Caro Campbell pressed the rolled paper into Mr. Veenstra's fingers and he thanked her, shifting the roll from hand to hand.

Bonnie saw her mother's eyes harden. "Do open it Nick," she said sweetly, and Mr. Veenstra's gaze met hers. Suddenly his face was as white as it had been red.

He hesitated, but Bonnie's mother reached out and drew the gold band off for him. Now he could do nothing but continue. His hands shaking, he slowly unrolled the paper.

"He knows we're on to him," whispered Bobbie, and Bonnie nodded, smiling, her heart pounding.

Aloud he read, "With thanks and appreciation from the residents of Mermaid Island, for your contributions to preserving our environment."

Most people in the room didn't see him pluck several copies of Moonie's photographs, stuck lightly with two-sided tape, off the certificate and slip them rapidly into his pocket. "We have the originals in a safe place" was written on the backs.

For a long time, Mr. Veenstra stood with his eyes downward, Caro Campbell standing next to him and glaring fiercely. Then he looked at the crowd and managed a thin smile.

"Thank you, everyone," he croaked. He cleared his throat. "You know…maybe it isn't necessary to go into this proposal for Yeoman's in such detail. We know what we want. We can vote right now."

The other members of the council were staring at him, open-mouthed, and Mrs. Veenstra was frowning slightly. Bonnie's mother pressed the other certificate into Mr. Veenstra's hand.

"Pass that on to Mr. McNaughton," she said, "I know he'll prize it as much as you do."

Mr. Veenstra spared her a vicious look, but continued speaking, "This island has always protected its natural habitats as its most important resource. I say 'NO!' to the Yeoman's development!"

The councilmembers were murmuring among themselves and looking in confusion at Mr. Veenstra, but one by one they agreed, each one voting "no" as the vote spread around the table. Clearly they had been expecting something very different from their chairman, and no one knew just what to do.

But the Mermaid Island residents hadn't waited for the end of the vote. They were streaming out of the hot, crowded room into the street, clapping, cheering and chattering noisily.

Bonnie and Moonie and Bobbie were hugging each other, the two VanGelderen brothers were hugging each other, and behind them Mrs. Veenstra was hugging Mr. Veenstra.

The VanGelderens all made their way to the back yard of the Campbells' tiny cabin where a barbecue was set up, and they stayed on into the wee hours of the night, telling and re-telling the story, and stuffing themselves to bursting on hamburgers and marshmallows.

As the final rays of the sun disappeared beyond the distant horizon, Bonnie found a moment to slip away from the party. Quickly, she went to the beach and stood gazing out at the water. There the mermaid waited, smiling her sweet smile, her milky white arms resting on top of the tossing water as if she were lying on the cushions of a huge bed. Green lights twinkled in her silver hair.

"All is well?" she asked, in her strange voice.

"All is well," answered Bonnie. "All is very, very well."

19

Bonnie waved until her arm and hand were numb, and didn't leave the rail of the ferry even though the distant figures of Bobbie and Moonie had faded into specks.

The summer was over, and Bonnie and her mother were heading back to the mainland. Bonnie was preparing to go back to school, and her mom would finish writing her research paper so she could submit it for publication. Caro Campbell joined her daughter at the railing and gazed at the faraway dock.

Bonnie had given each of her friends a pendant shaped like a mermaid holding a colored stone. The stone in Bobbie's was a bright red like her hair. Moonie's was an opalescent blue like a moonstone. Both girls were wearing them as they hugged each other good-bye on the dock, and Bonnie shed a few tears, though they were happy ones.

"You'll miss them," Bonnie's mother said.

"Yes," answered Bonnie, "but we'll write and email. And best of all, there's next summer!"

"Very true," answered her mother, smiling at Bonnie. "I left the deposit for the cabin with the caretaker when I left. We'll come back just as soon as school is out next June."

Bonnie grinned happily, then returned her gaze to the water.

"Do you suppose Mr. Veenstra gave the other thank-you certificate and the photos to Gregor McNaughton?" she asked.

"I don't know," her mother answered. She crossed her arms on the railing and brushed some strands of her blonde hair back from her face. "He sure looked surprised, didn't he? And we found a way to stop him without hurting his wife. He'll never be re-elected, though. She'll have to have a husband not on the Village Council."

"The VanGelderens will see to that," chimed in Bonnie.

"Right-o," said her mother. She put her hand on Bonnie's shoulder. "This has been quite a summer, hasn't it?"

"It sure has," said Bonnie. "Nothing turned out the way I thought it would. I made two great new friends, I have a new drink favorite..."

Her mother smiled.

"And I fell in love with Mermaid Island just like you did when you were a child. Can we come back every summer?"

"You don't have to ask me twice," answered Bonnie's mom. "We're all set for next summer, and I know we can rent our cabin whenever we like."

Caro Campbell went to curl up in one of the deck chairs, tucking up her sandaled feet and resting her chin on her knees to look toward the mainland.

Bonnie returned to watching the island. Now she could see Yeoman's Beach as the ferry chugged southward, the white sand seemingly endless. It sparkled gemlike in the bright sunshine.

In the distance, near the old log she had visited so often, she suddenly saw colors begin to gather and grow, swelling to aqua in the center. Out of the swirling water, the mermaid's pale shoulders arose, and Bonnie could see her silver hair spreading over the tips of the waves. Smiling her gentle, sweet smile, she raised one white hand in farewell, and Bonnie saw her tail flash golden, jade, and indigo beneath the crests of the waves.

Bonnie closed her fingers around the pearl at her throat and held tightly to the warm gem.

"I'll be back," Bonnie whispered into the wind. "See you next summer!"

More books by Judith Wade

The Memaid Island Series:

The Mermaid's Gift
Mermaid Dreams

Also by Judith Wade:

Faelen, The Horse from the Sea

For information on how to order, please visit:

http://rileypress.hypermart.net

or visit

Amazon.com

Have you ever seen a mermaid?

Most people think mermaids are imaginary, although it is fun to think and to write about what they might look like. But did you know that there are creatures living right here in the United States that sailors may once have mistaken for mermaids?

They're manatees, gentle, slow-moving mammals that eat submerged and floating grass and communicate with other manatees through chirps, whistles or squeaks.

The Florida manatee lives in the waters off Florida's coast. Other types of manatees live in the Caribbean, off the coast of Central and South America, and in the waters near West Africa. Sadly, manatees are an endangered species, partly because they can be injured or killed so easily by the propellers on motorized boats.

Manatees could use your help. There are several organizations that are dedicated to helping save the manatee. You can find out more information about the manatee by visiting:

http://www.savethemanatee.org

About the Author

Judith Wade lives in Michigan with her family, including her husband and daughter, dogs, cats, guinea pigs, fish and an ex-racehorse.

She loves to ride horseback, do stained glass, play in her garden and, of course, write.

Yes, one of her dogs is a pug.

You can email Judith Wade at: *jwadewrites@yahoo.com*